# MICHASO

## E. A. Padilla

# Michaso
## E. A. Padilla

EAP Publishing
eappublishing.com

Copyright © 2016 E. A. Padilla
ISBN 978-0-9964818-3-0
First Edition 2016

**PUBLISHER'S NOTE**

This novel is a work of fiction. Names, characters, and incidents are a product of the author's imagination. Any resemblance to actual persons, living or dead, or actual events, is entirely coincidental.

# Dedication

A special thanks to my friends who volunteered the use of their name(s) for my book; Reginald Chambers, Annalisa Barber-Gleason, Barbara Sivesind Fullem, the Ben Ano Nuevo family, and Greg Offord. Also to Rick Sarmento for helping with some statistical research; to Michele Hess for writing the review on the back of the book; and to my mother, Clara Neebling, for her painting that was used on the cover; and to my sister, Gordi Moeller, for taking the head shot photos.

# 1

She sat staring at the painting. The cold metal chair was bolted to the floor. Oblivious of her surroundings, she enjoyed the isolation. For a brief period after being hospitalized, she had remained under constant watch. Only once was she forced into a straightjacket. Her psychiatric evaluations were going deep beyond the circumstances of her life.

After several months, a custodian observed a crucial piece of information. While returning to her room to mop up a spill, he watched her transferring liquid from the floor to a bed sheet. She had draped it over a small table, creating a makeshift canvas, and she was painting what appeared to be a landscape. Keeping out of her view, he watched her mix water with dust from the window sill, and the green liquid soap from the sink, creating colors. These crude paints gave the picture a unique quality. From the doorway, he was taken aback by the change in her behavior, posture, and facial expressions. As a trained observer, he noticed the woman tilting her head, as if admiring her results. She held her index finger in the air, like an artist with an expensive paintbrush.

It was a breakthrough. From those observations, the medical staff found a potential opening into her psyche. It was the first time she had smiled since entering the hospital. She was an artist.

The staff created a private art studio out of one of the larger rooms. It was made available exclusively for this patient. During the day, she was given unlimited access.

As a self-admitted patient, she was held to a different protocol. Although she never checked out, she had the liberty to come and go as she pleased. All the necessary arrangements had been made. Her payments were regular and preauthorized. The money streamed in automatically. The staff surmised that she had to be wealthy. For the time being, she decided to stay. She was a special guest.

Any skepticism surrounding the wisdom of building the art studio was short lived. Upon entering the studio and seeing the art supplies, without hesitation she picked up a thick plastic safety paintbrush and prepared the colors. It became her daily routine, spending most of her available time in this room. The first painting was a maternity ward showing three babies, a young girl surrounded by two boys. The significance of that painting would be soon be discovered by an intern later that day.

During her counseling sessions, she spoke single-word responses. Having little to go on, the medical staff spent much energy analyzing her paintings. The principal question was how much of her art expressed her subconscious thoughts. Each painting was analyzed. Why did she paint a house perched near a cliff, with large, powerful waves crashing onto a jagged shoreline? Debate among the doctors centered on the significance of the sun. Was it rising or falling? The artwork was the only means in which her current state of mind could be ascertained. It didn't go unnoticed that only the first painting had included people. Since that time, she had painted only objects. The staff felt that allowing her to paint offered a limited but meaningful way of communicating. It would be their job to interpret these impressions and determine how to apply them to her situation.

Encouraging her to express herself through art caused an explosion of activity. Her finished paintings began covering the studio walls. In time, the subject matter within her art began to change. As if in synch, so did her behaviors. Her suicide attempts disappeared. She had somehow adapted to her self-imposed isolation. Her paintings reflected an opening up of her soul. Likewise, her counseling sessions began to change. She began to speak in full sentences. She became less resistant to explore her past. Although the retelling of her experiences lacked an emotional quality, the staff began plotting the road she had traveled; they hoped to eventually discover what event had caused her collapse. They knew the process and began peeling back the layers of her subconscious to expose the secrets she felt compelled to hide. The goal was to help her resolve the issues that had devastated her life. The art seemed to allow her a way to escape from her current circumstances. With time, her emotions began coming forward. Something deeper was being communicated. This process was giving her the strength to verbalize her past, helping her deal with the pain she had buried deep within herself.

Progress was slow. It took months before she began sharing anything significant, and what she shared brought little clarity to explain what led her to this point. The story thus far had been uneventful. The administrator believed that it must have been a cumulative effect. They were confident that someday she could resolve whatever continued to haunt her. It had taken her eighteen months in this mental facility to begin the healing process. This is her story.

\*     \*     \*     \*     \*

The newest intern sat at attention in a cold metal chair. It was his first day, and his excitement made it difficult to concentrate. Waiting to meet his new boss, he noticed a room across the hall where paintings covered the walls. As the inner office door opened, a woman's reflection bounced off a large safety-glazed window like a mirror. Her face was peaceful, and she had straight, thin lips. She appeared to be a caring person. The intern pondered what a person like that was doing in this place. She was very attractive and looked to be of Asian descent. As the door swung shut, her beautiful reflection disappeared. The intern craned his neck, trying to sneak another peak into the art room. She was remarkable. Equally impressive were the paintings, which matched her stunning beauty. He couldn't help but admire both. It would be many months before the intern would recognize her work. Prior to her arrival here, several of her pieces had made their way into mass production through different advertising agencies. As the intern continued to wait, his thoughts were dominated by this patient. Who was she? He was somehow drawn to her.

His train of thought was broken as the administrator burst open the door, interrupting the intern's isolation. After exchanging introductions, the intern was taken on a tour of the facility. He was introduced to his co-workers, assigned a locker, and issued an identification badge. Then he was given a magnetic security key and left alone to dress into his green scrubs. As the intern pushed his arms through the sleeves his thoughts returned to the woman. What was her story? What had happened to her?

The intern's supervisor rapped her knuckles on the solid wooden door, and the noise echoed throughout the locker room. "Are you ready yet?" she yelled.

Slipping into his issued string-less deck shoes, he slammed the locker door shut, preparing for the first day of his internship. He wanted to be accepted into a medical school, and he knew the competition would be fierce. Having an internship at a mental hospital the size of Long Beach was a feather in his cap and would definitely improve his chances.

Exiting the locker room, the intern followed his supervisor toward the cafeteria. As they paced down the hallway, he again saw the woman. He speculated that she must be finishing her latest painting. Frozen motionless, she sat staring at the painting. It was a portrait of a man. As the intern continued to pace around the corner, the woman tilted her head, as if trying to identify the person from only the sound of the footsteps echoing in the hallway. Turning toward the sound, the patient's attention was drawn to the intern. For a brief moment, they made eye contact. The intern noticed a single teardrop rolling down her face. He felt like an intruder. Her expression was intense. In that brief moment, he could almost feel her pain, as if her life was filled with despair, dominated by agony. No complicated tests were necessary. Any person looking into her face could detect her torment, her anguish. She was trapped inside of her mind. She was a lost soul.

The intern continued down the hallway in a quickened pace, chasing after his supervisor. Her distorted image was broken as the glass barrier ended and was replaced by the sanitary whitewashed walls of the facility. Pushing the heavy doors open, he allowed his thoughts to return to the woman with the paintings, hoping that he would get the chance to learn more about her. The double doors slammed as the automatic locks engaged.

\* \* \* \* \*

Through brief interactions with the other staff members, the intern learned that the woman seldom spoke, choosing to communicate through delicate hand gestures. She expressed her moods through polite nods of her head and minute facial changes. He was shocked to hear that she almost beat another patient to death with a folding chair for touching her painting aisle; it was no surprise that the other patients avoided her. During her initial days at the facility, he was told, her outbursts—explosions of shrieks and commands in her native Korean tongue—revealed the fury that was trapped within. To delve deep into her psychological past, the staff would have to deal with her emotional and physical strength—attributes that worked against her. She was trapped by her memories, tormented by guilt, held captive by her own strong spirit. Her life was a tragedy yet to be understood.

The intern was elated to learn that it was the administrator's initiation process to allow every intern access to her psychiatric file. It avoided the persistent human curiosity that without fail had captured everyone on staff. She was a distraction that could not be ignored. As such, like the others before him, the intern was allowed a peek into a clinical recounting of her situation.

Her file was unimpressive. The folder was thinner than expected. The personal history was typed out on a single piece of paper. No husband, no boyfriend and no children. She had immigrated to the US from Seoul, South Korea, and spoke limited English. She had admitted herself into the hospital eighteen months earlier and to date there had been no visitors. He was disappointed. The most detailed accounting was the tab labeled "ART." Each of her paintings had been photographed and then a bullet-point analysis followed. She had completed twenty-eight paintings and was working on her twenty-ninth.

As the intern closed the file, he leaned back in his chair, stretching his neck and shoulders. He pursed his lips in confusion. Learning her past did little to clarify how she ended up a voluntary guest in the Long Beach Psychiatric Ward. The biggest question remained: Why did she fall so far from where she had been heading?

\* \* \* \* \*

The patient had noticed another new face. She'd seen many new employees over the months. She had adapted to her celebrity status and expected the curious looks. The stares and awkward glances had become commonplace. Glancing away from her newest painting, she could see the most recent intern, whose bright new scrubs betrayed his identity. Today, she was more focused. Today was what would have been her anniversary for a wedding that was supposed to have taken place at four o'clock. She recalled how she had made all her necessary arrangements. As her mind drifted back to the present, her eyes locked onto the intern as he scurried by her room. He craned his neck to get a better view through the safety glass. It was something about his body position, his facial expression—he looked just like the attendant from the catering service. The intern continued down the hallway, his figure disappearing beyond the window opening. Her imagination filled in the missing visual data and recreated the picture. Drifting back through her memories of that horrible day, she relived, in high definition, the images that had burned into her mind. As her brain began accessing those memories, her wakeful body froze into a catatonic stupor. Sitting upright, frozen in a sitting position, she held a paintbrush with a tight fisted grip. Her eyes closed as the memories flooded into her consciousness.

*"Aren't those flowers lovely?"*

*All the bridesmaids turned their attention as the catering assistant shuffled past the window carrying a large vase. The long-stemmed white roses overflowed the large oversized glass vase. As he disappeared beyond their view, they returned their attention to Hye-Jin.*

*With a controlled smile, she studied her reflection in the mirror. Glancing up, she admired the traditional Korean attire draped on the hanger. They had agreed to perform the ceremony twice, first in the American traditional dress and format, followed by the traditional Korean ceremony. The dual ceremony had become the standard procedure for mixed culture marriages.*

As she relived those memories of that day, it brought out emotions of elation with an underlying feeling of dread that lingered just out of her consciousness. It was a sense of despair, drifting below like a body of water covered by a hard, thin layer of ice; such a fragile barrier cover, ready to entrap anyone foolish enough to venture out onto the surface.

A solid wood door swung back into its closed and locked position, disrupting her thoughts. A sound erupted down the hallway. Holding her breath, her eyelids fluttered as she awoke from her trance. As her upper and lower eyelashes separated, her sad eyes were unveiled. Still frozen in a sitting position, holding the paintbrush, her chest began to recede as she breathed. Glancing up at the metal-cage-encased wall clock, she began to wonder what her final breakfast would be. What would it taste like? Would she be hungry?

The attendants had already begun to organize the cafeteria. Only those confined to their rooms or physically incapable of feeding themselves were fed in their rooms, separated from everyone else. It was the hospital's position that the social benefits of communal dining created an environment of inclusion, trust, and companionship that opened up some patients' psyche—creating an environment to help reformat prior memories that held people captive in their own fear—their own self-deprecating emotions of guilt and shame.

She bit down on the inside of her cheek. She didn't draw blood, but it was hard enough to keep her in the present. Over the months, she had learned this trick. It helped her fight through the effects of her medication. There was no real pain, just silence, a quiet calm. She glanced back at the aisle and looked back at the face she had been painting. Only the eyes remained unfinished. She had saved them for last. She couldn't bear to see his reflection. She couldn't stand the guilt she felt. It was all her fault. She dipped the brush into the paint, preparing to start on the eyes.

Admiring the portrait, she knew today was the day. Only later would it all make sense. It was the portrait of a man she had watched die; a man who loved her in his own way.

Sitting on her bed, she looked out the window, gazing off into the horizon. She would enjoy this breakfast. After all the years living in America, she had finally acquired the taste for eggs, toast, coffee, and orange juice. She still couldn't stomach the bacon, though; it was just too salty. It was 8:05 a.m. She had twelve hours left. She was certain that today would be the day. She was determined to make it happen. She was more motivated today. She was certain. She would follow through with it this time. Today would be her last day.

# 2

He had heard about a popular Korean restaurant and wanted to give it a try. As he walked through the doors, he sensed something different. Each booth had its own personalized barbecue with its own exhaust system overhead. Soft, soothing instrumental music filled the air. The music seemed uniquely Asian and, as he listened more closely, he knew for sure it was Korean. He'd been to many restaurants in Koreatown and felt this one had that same distinct cultural experience of the others. There was no doubt in his mind that it would be authentic. As expected, the receptionist was Korean. He examined her delicate features as she escorted him to his table and could distinguish the differences immediately. Koreans had the same attention to detail as the Japanese, and similar physical features to those of the Chinese, but Koreans tended to have softer, gentler features with an atomic explosive short anger fuse that could flare up to surprise the unsuspecting. Looking around, Cameron noticed that the busboys were also Korean. Glancing through the kitchen pass through, he could see that the cooks were as well. In fact, everyone in the restaurant was Korean except him. As the staff spoke to one another, they only spoke Korean. He loved the culture and felt like he had ventured into a different country, but only had to travel several miles into Wilshire Boulevard to enter this unique place in the US, right in the middle of sprawling Los Angeles.

Cameron reviewed the menu. Rather than pronouncing the name of the dish he wanted, which he could do fluently, he pointed at the picture. It looked like paper thin slices of beef. Before walking away, the waitress adjusted the knobs and stoked up the gas grill positioned in the center of his table. The grill began to steam as it warmed. She laid a knife and fork wrapped in a paper napkin in front of him. She guessed wrong. He could use chopsticks like he had been born in the Orient. Another server brought numerous small dishes, each containing a different vegetable arrangement. He knew that these small dishes were like Korean hors d'oeuvres.

Next to his table, he read a framed newspaper article that was nailed to the wall. It was titled "How she did it." The article ran under a photograph of the front of the restaurant. Cameron began to read.

*   *   *   *   *

*The owner of the new Shangri La Restaurant is a self-made woman. Like most immigrants, she possesses an inner confidence. Leaving the safety of her homeland, Hye-Jin Kim began her adventure, taking the first steps toward a new life. She arrived in a section of Los Angeles referred to as America's Seoul. The area of Los Angeles is densely populated by Koreans. The ten-block area off Wilshire Blvd is rich with their culture and dominated by their native language. LA's Korea Town could be any subdivision in one of Korea's biggest cities. The street signs, newspapers, people and customers communicate in their native Korean language. With determination and drive, she pursued the opportunities available in our capitalistic society. Like most Asian immigrants, she brought her entire savings, an amount* considered normal for a typical Korean coming to America, but far exceeding what most Americans will save during one's life time.

Within months of her arrival to the US, she began her pursuit to open her own restaurant. It was natural for her and other Korean immigrants to band together to help each other. The momentum, dreams and aspirations of these individuals gives them a competitive advantage in business as they band together, sharing their experiences and allowing them to refine their collective decision-making skills. Their collective energies helped create a pool of knowledge that when shared streamlines the process and demystifies traditional fears thus increasing the likelihood of success. While the idea of capitalism fans dreams, real success is measured by tangible results. Business the world over rewards those who make the best choices that result in successful outcomes. As these immigrants learn to adapt, working together and sharing their experiences makes the difference. And because of the American dream, most immigrants share the same goal. As each wave of immigrants arrive, their competitive advantage and decision to work collectively reinforces the need to form relationships.

This concept may have been engrained in the Korean psyche thousands of years before they began coming to America. Combining this single-minded desire to succeed with their long history of being sandwiched between two very aggressive countries—China and Japan—may have given these immigrants an advantage, a historical predisposition to succeed. The centuries of being isolated, being unable to rely on anyone else, forced Korea to contemplate new ideas and new solutions. This essential ingredient allowed Korea to literally survive for thousands of years defending the country and literally avoiding annihilation.

Over the years, Los Angeles has seen new dry cleaners, sushi restaurants, tailors, liquor stores, thrift stores and massage parlors, all owned by Koreans. They share common traits: self-reliance, self-employment, and the empowerment gained from controlling one's destiny.

*Wasting no time, Hye-Jin Kim began the process to become an American citizen. After years of waiting and subjecting herself to the mandatory interviews and questionnaires, her journey was completed one late summer afternoon. With 5,004 attendees, she strode across the concrete walkways of the Staple Center as she went through the ceremony. With her newfound enthusiasm, she promised to do what she could to assist her fellow countrymen succeed in America.*

*As Korean immigrants continued to enter Los Angeles, Hye-Jin Kim was determined more than ever to help her newly transplanted countrymen. She was fortunate to be in the right place at the right time: Taking advantage of a downturn in Southern California real estate, she purchased the location for her restaurant while living above in the second-floor apartments while renting small studio apartments inside the remaining section of the building to newly arriving Koreans.*

*It seemed fitting that in her native language, America is pronounced* Migug *which literally translates into* The Great Country. *After just four years, she has become a self-made business woman and continues to help others realize the American dream.*

\*    \*    \*    \*    \*

Hearing the kitchen pass-through door open, Cameron turned away from the newspaper article. He saw a short woman, maybe five feet, two inches tall. She exhibited a sense of confidence. Her face had sharp features. She had long straight black hair that hung to her waist. As she walked by Cameron's table, she looked into his eyes and paused.

"How are you?" she asked.

"Fine," replied Cameron, caught off guard by her directness.

"Thank you for coming to my restaurant. Is this your first visit here?"

"Yes it is."

Exchanging looks, she broke the awkward pause in the conversation. "I appreciate your business. I hope you enjoy your meal." With a slight bow of her head, she turned and continued walking toward the front door.

Cameron was taken back. She had a certain strength about her. Hearing her voice and seeing her pleasant smile, he felt captivated and drawn to her personality. Her spoken English was clear, but she possessed a slight accent with her *r's* and *l's*. Even with the accent, she was easy to understand. Although he could speak basic Korean, he didn't let it be known. As he thought about it, no one knew. He was private and just didn't share those personal things about himself with others. Until that moment, he had never considered the pursuit of an Asian woman. It had been years since he failed to vet a female he met. This encounter had somehow disarmed him. His normal reflexes and thought process, for some reason, hadn't kicked in. He was genuinely interested in this woman as a person.

Cameron continued to watch her as she walked through the front door. As it closed, he turned his attention back to his food, making a conscious note to himself. He wanted to get to know this woman.

* * * * *

Lounging on his worn cloth-covered sofa, Cameron's legs were propped up on his glass-topped coffee table as he watched CNN on his wall-mounted wide-screen TV. His home was sparsely decorated; clean and organized, to the point of being sterile and boring. Only after a closer examination would anyone have noticed that there were no photos of family or friends. He had no children or pets.

During commercials, he glanced over toward the fireplace. Out in the open, three objects were hidden in plain view. They represented his life's achievements, at least up to this point. A large sculpture of an Egyptian cat sat on the mantel, as if it were surveying the living room. It looked ordinary, like something one would buy at a garage sale. It appeared to be made of some dark, smooth wood.

His other treasures were framed above the mantel, permanently screwed into the drywall. The treasures were covered with Plexiglas rather than glass. Cameron didn't want to risk the glass breaking and damaging the painting that was hidden behind the poster he'd bought at the local religious book store. In a subtle act of defiance, he chose the mass-produced poster with a bible excerpt, superimposed on top of a picture of footprint impressions on a wet sandy beach. Hidden behind that poster was a Van Gogh. Only his black market contact, his insurance company, and their art appraiser knew it existed. The frame looked like any ordinary metal frame that one would buy to protect a picture. It wasn't.

Those items represented Cameron's life's work. The cat statue was actually made of solid gold. It had been painted a dark brown to make it appear wood. It weighed forty pounds of solid gold. At $1,100 per ounce, the statue represented over $700,000. The Van Gogh was titled *Country Lane with Two Figures* and was appraised at $697,000—the amount it had last sold for. The nondescript frame was solid platinum, weighing two pounds. The icing on the cake was the two three-carat diamonds, taken from his two prior wives' engagement rings, embedded in the top corners of the frame. Cameron's secret stash had a value of over $1.4 million dollars.

He had thought long and hard how to hide his bounty. If he converted his treasures into cash, he could avoid paying capital gains. They were commodities. If he had to pick up and go at a whim, he could put the cat and the picture in his car and leave everything else behind. If there was a fire, the painting was insured and his other items would survive, albeit somewhat toasted. They were objects that no thief would take and no person would see as having any real value. If he needed some money, he could literally sell one of the diamonds or chuck off pieces of his precious metal selling it by the ounce.

As the television commercial returned to the *CNN* broadcast, Cameron turned away from the fireplace. He couldn't help but smile. Posing as a high school teacher, and choosing to live in a modest three–bedroom, two-bath, 1,400 square foot home, he knew no one could have guessed his past, his wealth, and the fact that he was a cold-blooded killer.

*     *     *     *     *

His fourth period had just concluded. Following his normal routine, he went to the faculty lounge, grabbed his lunch from the refrigerator, and poured a cup of hot coffee before sitting at one of the tables. Each morning, he would go to Subway and get a sandwich and two cookies. Today it was going to be roast beef, following his normal rotation. Cameron never tired of *Subway* sandwiches.

He placed his retirement financial statement strategically on the table knowing that most people would not be able to help themselves. He was right. Everyone tried to sneak a peek at their values. It was human curiosity.

This week was the annual retirement workshop. It gave each teacher time to review their goals and meet the next lucky financial planner who was selected from a rotating list. These volunteers would share their expertise to the faculty, motivated by dreams of starting a few new plans or better yet, transferring a sizeable account away from his competitors and into investments that he could manage. Like clockwork, Cameron knew that from years past, the rumor mill had spread the word that good old Cameron had a nice nest egg. He had been recognized by past planners as being one of the few who had set a plan in motion many years ago and hadn't deviated from it. In reality, that wasn't the case. After the death of his first wife, he purchased a new house, paying cash with the life insurance proceeds. His second wife had a significant 401(k) that he received as the beneficiary. He used those funds, as well as the proceeds from her modest life insurance policy, to kick start his own retirement.

No one here knew he hadn't been saving his money, none of it, until after the passing of his first wife. Given the suspicious nature of her accidental overdose, Cameron had cut ties with their friends. He couldn't take all the sideway glances and hushed conversations. Even her family had openly discussed their disbelief in the way she died, almost but not quite coming out and accusing him of having something to do with it. There were no children, so over time, with a strategic plan, Cameron just slipped away. He never initiated any calls to her family and never reciprocated with birthday or Christmas cards. After moving, he never provided his forwarding address. Given that the authorities could find nothing to prove Cameron's involvement, even though he was considered a person of interest, no formal investigation against him could be made, and the case went cold. He quietly receded from that life, moving away from the Midwest to start a new one.

Cameron had never planned to do it. Over time, he had accepted the fact that he only cared about himself. He first noticed it as a child. Most people had empathy toward others. It was a natural emotion, but not for Cameron. He had no empathy. He truly didn't care. He only thought about his goals, his desires. He wasn't aggressive or mean natured. That was just how he was made. As a result, he never developed close friends and remained aloof, keeping others at arm's distance.

From an early age, others could detect his disconnect. Conversations with him were unusual and awkward. People eventually gave up trying to talk to him. Over time, Cameron's consistent mannerism had been established: He wouldn't expound or share his point of view; in most cases he held a blank stare, remaining quiet without interrupting. At first, people thought he was a good listener, taking in everything the other person was saying, politely waiting his turn to echo back an insightful reply to engage in a verbal exchange. But he never did that. Usually, it resulted in an awkward silence with a facial expression that suggested that he not only had nothing to say but also was experiencing excruciating physical discomfort at having to endure such a meaningless interaction. He just didn't care. Cameron was a narcissist.

In his mind, he was special and unique, believing others envied him. He had a sense of entitlement and exploited relationships as a means of manipulating people to achieve his goals. He was obsessed with accumulating wealth, at any cost. Over time, he stopped rationalizing his choices, accepting them as part of the plan. The fact that he hurt others was of no consequence. He had concluded that everyone, at some unknown time, would eventually die. He rationalized that he made sure their lives had meaning, by furthering his goals. Besides, these other people wanted him to be happy, right? They had said they loved him. What better sacrifice than for them to help him be that—happy. He hadn't forced them to list him as their beneficiary. They had done that of their own free will. This self-rationalization was what Cameron had told himself. And he believed it.

However, he failed to face the reality that he had manipulated his wives. He had created a false personality, only acting like a loving husband. He had never had any emotional association. He was playing a character. He had learned the behavior. Like an ongoing play, he molded his personality in a way that elicited the reactions he wanted. He even went so far as to pursue formal training in how to build better relationships, committing hours of training to learn these signs. He had developed those skills to the point that without thinking, he could maintain unwavering eye contact, leaning in toward a woman when she spoke, constantly nodding his head to acknowledge his engagement in the conversation. And, oh yes, a perfect smile. He had also mastered the art of timing in terms of gift giving for birthdays, Christmases, Valentine's Day, and anniversaries, taking hours to decide which card to send, making sure the proper emotion would be conveyed. He had learned it all, mastering those skills; knowing just what to say, how to say it, and when to say it. But unlike most people, those behaviors had no emotional context associated with them.

For normal people, acting this way is a sign of the strong emotional feelings one person has toward another. These outward signs of devotion imply that someone has positive feelings toward them. Witnessing firsthand these acts of selflessness helps create a belief and trust toward a person.

But with narcissists, none of that is true. A narcissist is so motivated at getting what he wants, that his decision to act this way has but one motivation—to gain others' trust, solely so they can be manipulated to help him achieve his goals, regardless of the consequences toward those being deceived. The worst part of the charade is that those being manipulated don't understand that the other person genuinely has no strong positive feelings toward them. The narcissist simply wants something from the other person. In Cameron's case, his obsession, his end game was wealth.

Cameron continued eating his roast beef sandwich and pretending to read a book. With every opportunity, he continued his pursuit of the next future wife, a person who could help him increase his financial portfolio. He watched out of the corner of his eye at people passing by his table trying to sneak a peek at his statement. He had purposely left the bottom-line balance in plain view for those who were interested.

Cameron had learned to smile, make eye contact and project a positive approachable demeanor, at the same time discreetly searching for any external signs of wealth. He was well versed on watches. Was it a knock-off or an original? You had to be careful. The Chinese had learned how to copy the sweeping second hand on *Rolex* watches. He was also proficient at evaluating diamonds. He could accurately assess diamonds' carat weight, color, and clarity. Were they real? Was it a VVS or an SI? He also had a good understanding of women's purses. He could spot a copy *Louis Vuitton* handbag a mile away. It was all in the high stitches per inch (SPI) and even in the well-matched and proportionate patterns.

He also knew the salary range of teachers in the entire state. He wasn't necessarily interested in another teacher, although it wasn't beyond the realm of possibility that one of them would work. Cameron had considered his best approach would be through an introduction to one of her friends. Maybe the husband of one of his colleagues had a promising occupation, perhaps belonging to a country club, law firm, or medicinal practice. If so, there must be friends in her social circle who were widowed or simply looking for a male companion. Securing this information was Cameron's goal. He didn't want to come out and ask her directly that type of approach would raise suspicions. He had already learned that lesson when his inquiries about someone got around. Besides, at this stage of his life, getting the information was part of the game. He believed he was better at this than most others. He wanted to savor the hunt. He was batting one hundred percent, two for two. But this time he wasn't going to settle for just anyone. He was in search of a whale.

# 3

Entering the faculty lounge, she sat down on the sofa. She had just returned from her car, as she had forgotten her financial and investment statements in the back seat of her newly leased *BMW* 755il. Her husband was a partner in a mid-sized law firm located down on Wilshire. The firm focused on real estate issues and estate planning. She had met her husband while attending the *University of Southern California*. He was in a fraternity, she was in a sorority. They hooked up during their junior year. After graduation, they attended Pepperdine University together. He was finishing his JD, and she was finishing her teaching credential. Once he landed his job at the firm and passed the bar exam, they moved to a nice apartment in the Palms area just off of Olympic. After several years, he made partner. They purchased a place in Malibu to enjoy the beach life.

Several years earlier, while driving toward her husband's firm, she had found a restaurant in nearby Koreatown. She loved the food and made it part of her weekly ritual. Over time, she met Hye-Jin, the owner of the restaurant. It wasn't long before they became good friends.

Cameron had been working on developing a solid relationship with Barbara for years. He kept track of her as she relaxed on the sofa. He already knew her story. In fact, he had done his research and knew her husband's résumé verbatim. He had narrowed down his options with the current faculty members, and she represented his best chance. He still had other options—one at *Gold's Gym* and another one from his church—but of the three, Barbara was his top choice.

"Hey, Barb! How have you been doing these days? Are you adjusting to the commute from Malibu?" he asked. He looked her directly in the eye, leaned forward, and waited for her rely.

"Oh, hi, Cameron. Yeah, we love it there. It's like the concrete disappears. It's so relaxing." Barbara rose from the couch and carried over a carry-out bag in one hand and her financial folder in the other. She sat down at the table with Cameron and noticed his statement balance. She couldn't help herself and took a sideways glance. *Wow, how could he save so much money on our salaries?* she thought.

Trying to redirect her glance from his paperwork, she let her eyes stray back toward Cameron, yet avoiding direct eye contact. Expecting her inward fear of being caught looking at his information, Cameron made sure to look down toward his sandwich, appearing to be concentrating on something else in the other direction. But he saw it all. He knew she had seen his balance, at least one of them.

"Do you mind if I sit and eat with you today, Cameron?" Barbara asked.

"Not at all," he said.

He took a napkin and wiped off the table, pulling his food closer to him, giving her more room than she needed. "Do you have enough room?" he asked, knowing the answer.

"Oh, yeah, fine. Sure," she replied. As she pulled out her food from the bag, she couldn't help but think what a nice guy Cameron was. He was always smiling and polite, and he had great eye contact. He would remember everything that she had told him previously, and she never felt like was hitting on her in any way. He would ask about her husband and never seemed to pry or be jealous about her circumstances. She understood that most of her colleagues didn't have the same situation, having a husband who was able to provide for her in this way. She knew she was lucky. With other faculty members, she could sense an underlying feeling of discontent, almost like competition, but not Cameron. In all honesty, he was probably better off financially than she was.

Barbara pulled out the food she had ordered from Hye-Jin's restaurant. It was a bowl of soup with a side order of thinly cut slices of barbecued pork ribs. It was a Korean dish called *galbi*. She extracted a set of chopsticks from a paper sleeve and snapped them apart. After removing any loose splinters by rubbing them together as if sharpening a knife, she began to eat. As Cameron looked at the food, he noticed the imprint on the chopstick sleeve. It was from the restaurant he had visited in Koreatown.

"I've eaten there before," remarked Cameron. "Isn't that the restaurant owned by that successful Korean woman? I recall reading an interesting article that was framed on one of the walls."

"Yeah, that's the place. The owner's name is Hye-Jin. She's a good friend of mine. We're taking painting classes together. She's a great artist," replied Barbara.

"I think I met her. I've only eaten there once. She came right up to my table and asked me about my food and thanked me for coming. She seemed very nice; extremely attractive, too." Cameron made a point of averting eye contact, hoping she'd take the bait.

Barbara sat watching Cameron squirm in his chair. She was sure that he was attracted to Hye-Jin, but he had too much class to come out and say anything. As she continued to eat her lunch, she thought they would make a good couple. Cameron was pleasant and good looking and had a nice nest egg saved up. He was probably still in his forties and had plenty of good years left. Although she didn't know that much about his personal life, she thought he could be a possibility. Turning her attention to the hot soup she had placed in the microwave, she made a mental note to talk to Hye-Jin about Cameron.

He watched her walk over to the microwave to retrieve her soup. He could tell that her heels were real Christian Louboutin Daffodile pumps. Her watch was an oyster perpetual Rolex with a smooth sweeping second hand. Her keychain laying on the table had the distinct blue and white propeller *BMW* logo. As she carried her hot bowl of soup back to the table, he couldn't miss her beautiful emerald cut solitaire diamond ring. It was white gold band, with a center stone that he guessed was just over 2.5 carats, definitely VSI or better. They were all real. Cameron was right, except for the ring. The diamond was bigger than he thought; it was 2.84 carats.

Cameron continued eating his sub sandwich and mentally switched gears. He needed to focus on Barbara. As he bit down on his food, it was like throwing a switch. His concentration turned toward exhibiting a positive self-image. All of those acting courses at the *LA City College* kicked in. All of those sales workshops he attended, even the Tony Robbins tapes had their effect. It was as if Cameron could transform like a chameleon changing colors as it walked across a changing landscape. Unlike the chameleon, though, Cameron stayed one color: a deep, dark black inside. He lacked any true emotional attachments to any person; instead, he had only a single-minded focus on materialistic riches.

\*     \*     \*     \*     \*

Mike was engaged in his nightly ritual. He had been sitting at his computer table for hours, scouring through various Internet searches. He was looking through *Facebook* and *LinkedIn* profiles, but nothing. He didn't have his brother-in-law's social security number, only his date of birth. It had been 10 years since his sister Annalisa had died. The coroner's report stated it was from an apparent prescription drug overdose, but he didn't believe it. Unknown to Michael, his sister's misfortune had been her marriage to Cameron. There was something that Mike had never liked about him.

Everyone else in their family had liked Annalisa's husband. Mike couldn't put his finger on it, but there was something about him that he didn't like. Mike believed it was as if her husband was always putting on a show, flashing a plastic smile and offering insincere words, but no one else saw but Mike. Only after Annalisa's passing did any of his other family members express any distrust toward her husband. In fact, a gathering on the Christmas following her death was the first time they had verbalized any concern as to whether she had truly died accidentally. Mike had been the only one there to come right out and accuse him. "Do you think he had anything to do with it?" He asked the others.

During that brief moment, all of the family members exchanged knowing glances, as if to ask each other in roll-call succession, as if each person present were mentally tallying up the votes. Timing is everything. At that exact moment, her husband had walked into the room. As the family members became aware of his presence, in unison, they each flinched inwardly, knowing he had heard what they were discussing. The following spring, it came as no surprise that he chose to move away. He also chose never to keep in contact or attempt to reunite with them on future family gatherings. He just vanished.

That awkward conversation had been brought up the next year. Twelve months had passed. The police investigation had closed. The authorities had said they had looked into the matter and concluded that, although her husband would have been their prime suspect, based on the lack of physical evidence, there was nothing to go on. Nothing could tie her husband to her overdose. The fact that Annalisa had been recovering from a back surgery and had been taking Opioids for years, starting with *Vicodin*, then progressing to *OxyContin* and then *Darvon*. The coroner had hypothesized that in many cases, where medication had been prescribed for chronic pain, many patients would unwittingly become addicted to the pain killers, while others would, over time, develop a high tolerance to the drug and require increased dosages. Although Annalisa had a similar case history, she had never showed any signs of developing a habit. She had not displayed any of the behaviors associated with an escalated addictive state.

As Mike continued searching for his sister's husband over the Internet, his thoughts drifted back to the week of her death. He specifically recalled her husband's telling him that Annalisa had been complaining about her back hurting her more than usual. But then Mike had bumped into her at the grocery store. He could remember that conversation as if it had taken place yesterday. When he asked Annalisa how she was feeling, she stated, "Fine, better than I've felt in years." Mike recalled being surprised at her response, given what he had been told, and pressed her further.

"You mean your back isn't bothering you?" Without hesitation, Annalisa replied "No. In fact, I've stopped taking my pills the last few days. I haven't needed them."

Over the years, he had replayed that conversation countless times. It had come to the point that he had memorized the words verbatim. At first, he thought that maybe she was exaggerating her medical condition and was hiding the fact that she had actually become addicted to the pain pills, given her apparent accidental overdose. Mike had become obsessed with her death. After years of contemplation, he was certain, regardless of the apparent evidence or of what anyone else thought, that he knew the truth. It was just one of those things that a person knows about a loved one.

And he was right. It called to mind the old adage that the harder a person works, the luckier he gets. Mike had devoted so much time and energy to one single passionate issue, that he reached a point where he was now capable of seeing things that others couldn't. His obsession had allowed him to accumulate enough skill, to become exposed to so much information, that he had reached a point where his efforts created a cumulative mastery that destined him to succeed. Mike had done his homework and thought through every angle. And he was absolutely one hundred percent correct—he just didn't know it yet.

It was past midnight. As usual, Mike had spent more time searching the Internet than he had planned. Mike had remained single, never marrying, and had no children. As he yanked downward on the pull chain to turn off the desk lamp, he kicked off his shoes and shuffled his way back to his bedroom. This routine had become his ritual. He had become obsessed with finding his sister's husband and having a heart-to-heart conversation with him about Annalisa. Still in his dirty athletic socks and stained t-shirt, Mike slid into his twin bed. The linen sheets were cold. As he turned onto his side, he looked out the window and gazed into the distance, waiting for sleep to come.

Mike's hunch was correct: Something had been wrong. She had not been taking her pills for the last six days before she died. What Mike didn't know was that this had given her husband an opportunity to stash the pills. There would be no reason for anyone to assume otherwise. He knew that the authorities would check her dosage and calculate if too many pills were missing. The prescription drugs had to be refilled, as they had been for years. If she took more than usual, it could easily be proved. But if the count was accurate, if there were the exact number of pills remaining until her next refill, there would be no red flags. No one would suspect anything. With this mindset, her husband had set his plan into motion.

With her normal dosage of two pills per day, he had twelve unaccounted-for pills. He crushed them into a fine powder and dispersed the drug to her in everything she ate that day. He put it into her capsulized multi-vitamin, added it to her morning orange juice, and added it to her coffee, buttered toast, and fried eggs. He had slipped it into her afternoon blended fruit shake and into her Caesar salad at lunch. He had laced it in with her mashed potatoes and gravy and inserted it inside her rib eye steak for dinner. He even had mixed it into her dessert cake and ice cream, as well as into her evening tea. To his shock, even with all of that, Annalisa had seemed normal and unaffected. Only after he had urged her to take a normal dose did it push her over the edge. Her husband had reminded Annalisa that she hadn't taken her medicine for six days and expressed his fear that by neglecting her medication she was overdoing it, and he was fearful that her back would pay the price over the following days. Because of her husband's concern for her well-being, she gave in to his concerns. To appease his fears, she offered to take a double dose, but he said that wouldn't be necessary. After going to bed that night, she never woke up.

Mike continued to toss and turn, trying to relax and fall asleep. As he closed his eyes, he thought to himself, "I must be missing something." Again, he was right. But all of his efforts, all of the hours he had devoted to her death, were about to pay off. It wouldn't be long now. Tomorrow was the day. He would uncover one small clue, a piece of the puzzle that no one else would deem important. He would uncover that one piece of data that could unravel everything. And it had been staring him in the face every day since that fateful day. Since her death, he had looked at it every day. But this time, what he saw would change the course of his life forever. Next to his computer he had placed a framed picture of his sister sitting on her husband's car. It was just a matter of time now.

# 4

The cafeteria at the school had been converted into a makeshift meeting area for the faculty's annual retirement meeting. Cameron had been one of the first ones there. He strategically sat in the back row so he could see everyone entering. He was hoping to see Barbara and her friend Hye-Jin. The teachers were allowed to bring their spouses, friends, and children. The school district understood that retirement affected a person's entire life and wanted everyone to be prepared.

During lunch the day before the meeting, Barbara had mentioned to Cameron that Hye-Jin might be coming. Just in case, he had dressed nicely, gotten a fresh haircut, and had avoided garlic and onions for dinner that night. He also boned up on his Korean; it had been a while since he had used it. Glancing through the large plate glass windows, he saw Barbara's white *BMW* roll past and park. Cameron stood and walked to the windows to get a better look. As the passenger door opened, he saw Hye-Jin. As they walked closer to the cafeteria, he became mesmerized, as if something altogether new was happening. All of his preplanning went out the window. He dropped his playbook and had no desire to orchestrate, manipulate, or control their meeting. For the first time in his entire life he was actually excited to meet someone, without having some inappropriate ulterior motive. For the first time, he found himself becoming nervous.

Unaccustomed to these new feelings, Cameron made his way back to his chair and waited for them to enter. Barbara entered first, with Hye-Jin right behind her. As they walked through the doorway into the meeting area, Barbara noticed Cameron waving her direction. "Oh, hi, Cameron," said Barbara. She was somewhat surprised by his demeanor. He seemed different. She had always found him to be nice, but in a clinical way. But for some reason, tonight, he seemed happy, sincerely happy, to see her. As she walked closer to Cameron, she formally introduced her friend.

"Cameron, this is Hye-Jin. Hye-Jin, this is Cameron." Looking at Hye-Jin, Barbara continued, "He mentioned that he had been at your restaurant and met you briefly there."

Hye-Jin had always been somewhat shy with American men, and she kept her eyes down, leaning her torso forward slightly and facing downward as if to avoid eye contact. With only a slight accent, she said, "Nice to meet you, Cameron," and extended her right hand.

Cameron stepped forward and, as if he had been speaking Korean for years, replied in her native tongue. "*Annyong haseyo, mannaso pangapsumnida*," he said, and reached out his hand while bowing as he shook her hand.

Both Barbara and Hye-Jin were taken aback. "You speak Korean?" Barbara asked.

"Only a little," Cameron replied.

"Wow, I had no idea, Cameron. You're full of surprises, aren't you?" said Barbara.

In times past, Cameron would have had a witty, preplanned comeback, a saying he had rehearsed, designed to elicit a specific reaction. But at this instant, he had no specific goal in mind. This time, for some reason, he paused and allowed himself to consider the question without a narcissistic filter. Turning his face toward Barbara, he smiled and replied, "I guess I am." During that brief exchange and pause in the conversation, all three exchanged glances. There seemed to be a comfortable connection between all three. Barbara thought, *Wow, what a surprise! Cameron is actually sensitive and approachable.* With that, Barbara took matters in her own hands.

"Do you mind if we sit with you?" she asked. Both women looked into Cameron's face for his response.

With a soft, comfortable warm smile, he replied, "I'd love it!" and backed away from the row of chairs, waving his hand encourage the women to enter the aisle. Both women smiled and took their seats next to him. Minutes later, the meeting began. All three sat listening to the speaker discuss strategies involving living trusts, life insurance, and the pros and cons of annuities. Another speaker seemed to specialize in real estate and discussed refinancing options, reverse mortgages, and taxes. The meeting continued for two hours without any formal breaks. The moderators knew better than to give their audience a chance to leave. During the presentation, questions were encouraged, and Cameron, Barbara, and Hye-Jin took copious notes.

As the meeting began to wrap up, Barbara leaned over to Cameron and whispered in his ear. "Hey, Cam, we're going out for a cup of coffee and a pastry afterward. Do you want to come along?"

Barbara looked into his eyes, waiting for his response. Cameron used one of his hands like a megaphone to muffle his reply. "That would be great. Where are you going?"

"Starbucks, on the corner."

Still whispering, he replied, "I'm in" and smiled back at her.

She had known Cameron for the last five years, and she couldn't recall ever feeling close to him, even though they had been having casual talks during lunch in the faculty lounge or during their other meetings. She had just considered him an acquaintance, someone she worked with. But tonight, she began to see a different side of him; a warm, approachable, and interesting man.

As the meeting concluded, the attendees began to exit. Cameron walked them to Barbara's car. Once Barbara was inside her car, she told Hye-Jin that Cameron was going to join them at the coffee shop.

"That's fine," replied Hye-Jin. "He seems like a nice guy. Did you know that he spoke Korean?"

"He is a nice guy. And I was surprised by that one. I had no clue."

"I wonder where he learned to speak Korean?" Hye-Jin interjected. Given his word choice, she was certain he hadn't learned it through casual contacts while in the military; his word usage was too formal and honorific.

They arrived at the coffee shop first and found a larger table, where they waited for Cameron. He was only a few minutes behind and walked in, scanning the room for the women. They waved to him, and he walked over with a comfortable, confident smile.

""Annyong haseyo? Anjo yogi demika?" he asked Hye-Jin. Smiling, she nodded her head and replied in English. "Sure, you can sit here," as she patted the chair next to her. Barbara couldn't wait any longer and blurted, "Where did you learn Korean, Cam?"

Without filtering his answer, he replied truthfully. "Several years ago, prior to moving to LA, I had taken a cruise. It was something I'd always wanted to do. After the passing of a relative, and during my transition in careers, I finally did it. It was an extended twenty-eight-day cruise throughout Asia. I was able to visit China, Cambodia, Vietnam, The Philippines, Japan, and, of course, Korea," He continued. "Because Korea and Japan are the most similar to the US in terms of modernization, I felt more comfortable making my starting and ending point in one of those two countries. I chose Korea."

"Why Korea?" asked Barbara.

"I'm not sure," he replied. "For some reason, I've always been fascinated with Korea."

"And learning to speak Korean?" asked Hye-Jin.

"Oh, yeah. I'm kind of OCD and wanted to be able to interact with the people, so I took some CD crash courses for each country. I was able to say 'hello,' 'nice to meet you,' 'may I sit here'—you know, the basics."

"You sound like you speak more than the basics," Hye-Jin added.

"After the cruise, I stayed two weeks in Seoul. So I had a longer exposure to the Korean culture than any of the other countries." Tilting his eyes upward as if searching for an explanation, Cameron looked Hye-Jin in the eye and continued, "There was something about that place that captured my spirit; the people, the culture, the food. I don't think I have any Korean ancestry in my bloodline," he chuckled. "Maybe I was Korean in my past life." He began to laugh. So did Barbara.

Hye-Jin didn't understand the joke and replied, "Past life? Do you believe in past lives?" asked Hye-Jin, eager to hear his reply.

Barbara interjected, "He's just joking! It's just an American saying, 'past life.'"

Hye-Jin smiled back, but she didn't really understand the joke. Although in present-day Korea, most of the people in South Korea were Christian, there remained an underlying cultural influence dating back thousands of years before Korea had become a country. There was a Buddhist influence which did believe in reincarnation; a belief that each person would face the prospect of reliving their life should it not be lived properly with honesty, integrity, and respect for every person. Hye-Jin was wondering whether Cameron was really joking.

Cameron stood up and offered to get everyone a coffee and a crumb cake. As he approached the counter, he thought, *Why did you tell them that?* Everything he had said was one-hundred-percent true, from start to finish. He began to chastise himself more. *Why did you do that? You never share anything about yourself. And, worse yet, you haven't done anything to manipulate the situation, nothing to win over Hye-Jin. You haven't even thought about evaluating her jewelry and clothes, or prying into her past to gain some insight into her finances. Even during the meeting, you didn't try to sneak a peek at her notes to see if she had written anything down about her net worth, her future plans. What are you doing?*

In all of his life, as far back as he could remember, he had never acted this way. This evening, he was honest, open, and sincerely interested in another person. He was torn between two emotions: anger and excitement.

Looking at Cameron standing at the counter, Barbara finally spoke. "Hye-Jin, I never knew that Cam was so worldly. He had never mentioned anything about traveling to Asia or speaking Korean. What a surprise, right?"

Hye-Jin smiled back, thinking that he was a private person, one who didn't need to brag. A quiet, silent type was a very attractive quality that most Korean women appreciated in a man. A man's silence suggested an inner strength and self-confidence. She nodded her head toward Barbara, acknowledging that she understood. She felt the need to visit the restroom. She had to pass Cameron on her way there. Cameron was still waiting for their order to be prepared. As she walked by, he noticed her approaching. With a slight smile, he leaned forward bowing at the waist in her direction as she passed. As a natural response, she paused and returned the bow. As she continued walking, she grew more impressed by his understanding of her culture and mannerisms.

As Cameron continued to wait for their order, he began to feel strong, unaccustomed emotions. He was relaxed, comfortable, and at peace. He wasn't preoccupied with gaining information about others. His mind wasn't dominated by thoughts of increasing his wealth. He was content and happy being in the present, spending time with ... friends. It was a first for him. As his order was called, he gathered the items and dropped a ten-dollar bill into the tip jar. Over-tipping was also a first. In times past, the best he tipped was the change that remained, rounding upward and then nothing to exceed ten percent. Never before had he ever left a thirty percent tip! Walking back to the table, Cameron couldn't help but smile. Something was happening. He just didn't know what it was.

* * * * *

Mike's neck was stiff. He closed his eyes again and wiped the drool from his mouth. He saw the wet spot on his pillow from sleeping with his mouth open. Yawning, he stretched his arms and sat up. It was one of the best solid nights of sleep he'd had in years. His socks were still on and he had serious morning breath; he hadn't brushed his teeth again before going to bed.

It had been years since he had awakened without thinking about his sister. He was hungrier than normal as it was almost 11:30 in the morning. It was Saturday, and he didn't have to worry about work. *NFL* Football would be on television all day tomorrow. Today he had nothing planned.

As Mike finished a quick pit stop in the bathroom, he sauntered into the kitchen, glancing at his computer table and the picture of his late sister Annalisa. It was the first time since her passing that her memory hadn't triggered a reaction, causing him to start to obsess over the suspicious nature of her death. He paused and admired her facial features and remembered her pleasant, positive attitude. He even acknowledged the beauty of Lee's 1967 *Ford Mustang*. It was the first time since her passing that he had looked at the picture and hadn't felt rage and hatred toward Lee. It wasn't that he had forgiven him, it was just that it was the first time in over ten years that he hadn't become furious when looking at the photograph; it hadn't triggered those compulsive painful memories. Mike had reached a point that the anger and pain had subsided, so that he hadn't clenched his fists in anger while the bad feelings, memories, and emotions pushed forward into his thoughts. He could actually admire the picture in its entirety without being consumed by rage.

Turning toward the kitchen, Mike felt lighthearted, smiling to himself and preparing for a pleasant day. It was the first time he had been happy since her passing. As he opened the refrigerator he grabbed a carton of milk, tilting it to check the expiration date. Holding the cold, moist carton reminded Mike about the time he had washed that beautiful *Ford Mustang* that Lee owned.

It was during that exact moment, that it hit him. The car! Like a perfect storm, Mike could finally unravel a clue that had been staring him in the face this entire time but, because of his prior mental state, he had missed it. The car.

Mike turned toward the computer desk. Jogging over, he picked up the picture frame and held it up to this face. "Of course!" he shouted, raising his hand in the air like Rocky Balboa as he reached the top of the concrete stairway. Mike's smile spread across his entire face. He turned back toward the refrigerator to return the milk and then sprinted toward his bedroom. Grabbing his sweatpants and jacket, Mike dressed, shoving the framed picture into a duffle bag, along with his wallet. Slipping into his boots, he grabbed his car keys and rushed out the front door. He had a new sense of energy, a new purpose, a new lead—the vehicle registration.

He had researched the license plate idea years before. What he learned back then was that the vehicle had apparently been sold by Lee Fullem and was now registered under a different name, not Lee's.

Years before, Mike didn't have any specific idea or theory. He just wanted to locate Lee. But now, after devoting so much time to thinking things through, he had decided that his first step was to locate Lee. To that end, he began thinking outside the box, considering unconventional ways to locate Lee's whereabouts. Prior, he would never have considered meeting the new owner of the car. He would never have contemplated taking it that far. But that was then, and this was now. He had reached a point where he didn't question his actions. He knew that to move on, he had to first locate Lee, and then have a face-to-face meeting. From there, he would improvise.

This idea was going to require him to take his commitment level to new heights. He was now all in in terms of locating Lee.

Even though the registration had not provided Lee's address, it gave him a logical starting point, another avenue of thinking. It made sense. If only he could meet the new owner of the Mustang, Mike could find out the circumstances of the purchase. It had to be a private-party purchase. There was a chance that the buyer had met Lee at some point during the transaction. With any luck, maybe they had met at Lee's house. With any luck, the current registered owner of the car was still the same person who had purchased the vehicle from Lee, not someone else. He needed that chain of custody to be clean; otherwise, it could lead to a dead end. If Mike's memory was accurate, his original research had shown the same address as his sister's. But what Mike didn't realize then was it was the name Cameron Sivesind that had thrown him off. He had expected to see Lee Fullem's name on the registration. Mike had assumed that Lee had sold the vehicle to this Cameron Sivesind person. He had missed the connection and had it all wrong. Annalisa's husband had gone by a different name when they were married. At the time of her marriage, her husband's name was Lee Fullem. What Mike had missed was why the newly registered owner, this Cameron Sivesind person, had used his sister's address. The name had thrown him off. In reality, Lee had simply updated the vehicle registration by using his new name of Cameron Sivesind when he first moved away. Now it was only a matter of time. Mike was onto something. But he needed help before it would all become clear.

One of Mike's best friends was a detective. The stereotypes were true. Those guys loved their donuts. He was heading over to the donut shop to get two dozen donuts. It was time for a full-court press, no holding back.

*     *     *     *     *

Mike walked into his friend's office carrying two dozen donuts. After closing the door behind him, he propped the box open and held it elevated so Chuck could see the whole spread. Mike extended the box out over Chuck's paper covered desk like a pizza on a tray that had just come out of the oven. His friend couldn't help but break a grin from ear to ear as he pushed back from his desk to stand, gladly accepting Mike's offering—well, bribe really.

"I've got your favorites, my friend," said Mike as he set the bulging box of assorted donuts on the wood desk top. "The twists and old fashioned chocolates and the cream-filled bars too, big guy," he added with a huge smile of his own.

"Damn Mike! You must be in deep shit if you're bringing me this much stuff. I told you before good buddy, just take traffic school. It's on the Internet now, for God's sake. Only take you couple of hours." Chuck's thick, pudgy fingers dove into the box, retrieving a cream-filled chocolate bar, and he devoured half of it in one bite. Only after several chomps into the donut did Chuck finally look up at Mike for a response.

"No, nothing like that. It's no biggie, but I just needed to get the information about my brother-in-law's old '67 Mustang." Mike replied. Choosing his words carefully, he proceeded. "I was just thinking that, you know, for old time's sake, I'd like to track down that car and buy it." Mike knew that Chuck had heard all of his prior theories about how her husband Lee had something to do with her accidental overdose and didn't want him to be concerned about him having any crazy thoughts. So he lied.

"Hmm." Chuck's gut told him Mike was probably lying. Why so many donuts? As he considered Mike's request, he could see a piece of paper in Mike's hand. He could just make out the numbers and knew right away it was a license plate number. Without letting Mike know what he was up to, Chuck began pulling up what information he could find. Then, depending on what information he uncovered about the last known owner of the car, Chuck would decide how to proceed. As Chuck leaned forward in his chair, he shoved the rest of his first donut into his mouth and chased it with a large swig from his oversized coffee mug. It was his ninth cup of black coffee this morning. With the skill of a cop with twenty years of experience, Chuck was able to shake his computer mouse and punch up the data, while distracting Mike with a facial expression that indicated he was still waiting for a response. Chuck knew that distracting Mike and leading him to believe he was waiting for a response would cause Mike to be self-conscious and begin to formulate his next words. That was all the distraction Chuck needed as he glanced back at the screen to see the most current information available on that vehicle. While still waiting for Mike's response, Chuck reached back into the box and grabbed an old-fashioned glazed donut this time, and took a bite. With crumbs stuck to the corner of his mouth, Chuck continued to wait.

"So what do you think?" asked Mike as some crumbles fell out of Chuck's mouth.

"Why do you have to have his car? Wouldn't any '67 *Ford Mustang* do? Why his?" pressed Chuck.

"You know, for some reason, losing Annalisa like that, so unexpectedly, I guess that car reminds me of her, in a good way. The happy times, before she died, you know?" replied Mike.

"I guess I understand," replied Chuck. He reached out his hand. "Let me see what you got there." Mike handed Chuck the piece of paper. Chuck took the paper and pushed several buttons on his keyboard. He was researching the last known registered owners that they had in their database, which wasn't Lee Fullem, thank goodness. The new name on the last registration had been transferred in the Nebraska DMV into the name of a Cameron Sivesind, who was in the process of moving to Los Angeles.

Mike watched Chuck punching his keyboard and clicking his mouse. He knew he was pushing their friendship by asking him to do this. But he couldn't help himself. He had been obsessed over Annalisa's death and had made some bold statements and shared some wild theories with Chuck during the early stages of the investigation. At the time of her overdose, Chuck was just a patrolman, handing out parking citations and speeding tickets in the city of Scottsbluff,

Nebraska. But today things were different. He was a captain and had aspirations of a transfer to Lincoln or Grand Isle. The last thing he needed was to be involved in an incident that started because he released sensitive private information.

"I'm sorry for asking, Chuck," offered Mike. "It's all harmless. I figured it would make me feel better if I had that car to remind me of the good times she had. Kinda stupid, I guess."

As Chuck listened to Mike, he began making some educated assumptions about the situation. Chuck contemplated the odds of this Cameron guy still having the car. If the car went to California, that was over ten years ago. Chuck rationalized that he had probably sold it by now. Heck, it could have been totaled in a car accident for all they knew. Looking up at Mike, he couldn't help but feel sorry for him. After all these years, still single, and still obsessed over what had happened to his sister, never being able to move on.

"You know what, buddy, I'll give you the information you want. I'm thinking it's a wild-ass-goose chase anyway. It's been ten years, Mike! You need to promise me something first. If I do you this solid, you're done, okay? No more inquiries about your sister's past. I understand, but man, you need to move on."

Chuck paused and stared Mike dead straight in the eyes. "You understand Mike. I'm worried about you. I'm guessing even with this information, it's a dead end." He paused and asked again. "I want to hear it Mike. You promise me right now."

Mike's head had remained tilted downward as he listened to Chuck, with his eyes closed in deep concentration. Mike knew Chuck was right. *What good will any of this information do, anyway,* he thought. But there was just one thing that he couldn't shake. It was the discrepancy about the last conversation he had with Annalisa. Why would she have lied? She had looked great. Her eyes were clear, she seemed happy, rejuvenated and free. Mike just didn't believe Lee. Mike was convinced that scumbag of a husband had something to do with her death. He just knew it. Sitting up tall in his chair, Mike returned Chuck's cold steely stare and replied, "I'm serious, Chuck. You help me out on this one and it will be done. If I can't find that car, I'll just buy another one like it and call it quits. I swear." And Mike was serious. He meant every word.

Reaching out across the desk, Chuck stretched out his strong right arm to seal the promise with a handshake. Mike exchanged a firm, sincere gesture as he shook Chuck's hand. A man's word is his bond. Without it, there's nothing. It's all about integrity.

With that, Chuck made his decision and pulled a blank piece of plain paper from the printer and hand-wrote the new owner's name, last known address and the VIN number. Chuck then handed the paper to Mike and said, "You never got this from me. If it gets out, I'll deny it to everyone who asks. And you might as well keep walking like we never met, 'cause I don't want this to come back to haunt me in any shape or form. So write this information in your own handwriting. Here's a piece of paper. Got it?"

Mike looked down at the paper and smiled. He wrote down the information on the back of the same piece of paper he brought and handed back to Chuck the paper with the information. Chuck shredded that paper while Mike pocketed his own paper and stood to leave. "Thanks Chuck. I'm serious. This is it. No more. I'm good. I just want something to remind me of her. If I can't find Lee's old car, then I'll get another one."

In speaking those words, Mike had been one hundred percent honest and truthful. It was only a matter of time before everything would change. Some things are better left alone. And this was one of those times.

# 5

Jonathan sat in his shiny new Mercedes S550. He was finishing a conference call with his Japanese counterpart in Tokyo. Every six months he had to cross the Pacific for a week-long corporate management meeting. He had grown to enjoy those trips. The cultural differences were a shock to most people's systems. Adjusting from the witty, overconfident, bordering–on-obnoxiousness of the Americans to the rigid face-saving restraint of the Japanese culture created a challenging work environment. Although many jokes were aimed at the Japanese for their accents, bowing, and overly ritualistic gestures and grunts, the fact remained that they were smart and creative. Their attention to detail, dogmatic work ethic, and absolute accountability at every level in their organizations spoke volumes about the superior quality of their finished products. It was a universal truth that *Sony, Toyota, Lexus and Yamaha* represented some of the highest quality products within their respective industries.

Like their work products, the people the Japanese chose to do business with also possessed a unique superior quality.

Being a success in a bicultural environment required an ability to assimilate between cultures and to possess strong language skills. Likewise, it required a patient, calculating mind. One needed the ability to swallow one's pride and literally carry the company flag at international intramural sporting events that took team building to a level never seen or understood by most Americans. As a project manager, Jonathan Weed had the responsibility to organize entire groups of professionals from within and outside of his company to rally them behind an idea or goal. These projects centered around concepts, while others focused on a physical product.

Jonathan adjusted the rearview mirror as he straightened his bushy mustache with his thumb and index finger. As a Caucasian American, he possessed a physical advantage. Compared to his Japanese counterpart, he was physically taller and bigger, with the ability to grow thick facial hair. He had discovered that most Asian men had an inferiority complex about these physical characteristics. As such, Jonathan believed that these traits gave him a psychological advantage.

Squinting at his reflection in the rearview mirror, Jonathan concentrated on the words blaring from his car's speaker phone. Jonathan preferred taking these weekly calls from his car. It was his environment. Knowing his compulsive nature, he preferred being isolated, away from the watchful eyes of his colleagues. The all-glass-windowed office building gave little protection from the wandering eyes of others. Inside his car, he was free. He could focus on his steering wheel, admiring the *Mercedes Benz* emblem. That always gave him strength. Before the call, he could blast *Van Halen or AC/DC*, preparing his mind for the intellectual battle ahead. The subtle noise that a leather chair makes when a seated person adjusts his weight was of no consequence. He could control his sitting position while stroking his mustache as many times as he wanted, without fear of criticism from his co-workers.

Jonathan understood that every call, every interaction, every report—everything that took place between Japan's home office representatives and anyone from the American office—was recorded. Afterward, it was scrutinized, dissected, and examined. From that first conference call, his superiors had warned him that every telephone call, regardless of the subject matter, would be taped. He suspected that upper management never relied on a verbal report from their representatives involved in those conversations. They trusted no one and always thought the worst, considered the unthinkable, and planned accordingly. His Japanese co-workers were so paranoid about conspiracy, back-room deals, and secrets that they even monitored their translators. To help combat the potential risk of corporate espionage, they required every vice president position and above to master English. As a result, those executives had a superior grasp of the English language, equivalent to that of students graduating with a Bachelor's degree from the United States. Nothing was left to chance; nothing was taken at face value—absolutely nothing. The idea of trust was a concept, an idea, propaganda. In Japan, everyone mistrusted everyone.

Prior to the conference call, Jonathan had discovered that during a company tournament, Yuri had a miserable round of golf. It was an unthinkable score of one hundred three. For an executive to have such a score was more than embarrassing. It could be a career breaker. As the meeting wound down, Jonathan made a point to highlight Yuri's golf failings.

"So, Yuri, I guess more hours are needed at the driving range, yes?"

A brief awkward silence fell on the other line. A slight cough of embarrassment echoed throughout the *Mercedes'* interior. Searching for a proper yet witty comeback, all Yuri could muster was a short direct response.

"I must have been too focused on this week's summit in Detroit. I'm sure my game will recover to the expected sub-eighties."

As Jonathan depressed the end button on his car phone, he simultaneously depressed the stop button on his tape recorder. Jonathan wasn't to be out done. Two could play the taping-conversation game. He did everything in his power to match their actions, tit for tat. Driving out of his reserved parking space, making a beeline to the nearest driving range, he whispered under his breath, "Is he really sub-eighty?"

\*   \*   \*   \*   \*

Hye-Jin sat at traffic court waiting for her number to be called. Then she saw him, a large-shouldered man with a bushy mustache. He wasn't particularly attractive, but there was something about him—the way he walked, his gestures. He held a thin, controlled smile and acknowledged others in a slow, bowing mannerism. Despite his polite, submissive demeanor, he projected strength and confidence—an agreeable nature.

After looking down the aisle of chairs, Jonathan noticed the woman. As he gazed upon this Asian goddess, he forgot why he had been obsessing over the speeding ticket. Prior to focusing his attention on this gorgeous beauty, he had been self-absorbed about fighting the ticket. It was a bogus speed trap at the bottom of a steep hill. The residential speed limit allowed for thirty-five miles per hour. Jonathan was obsessed with the idea that the only reason the twenty-five-MPH zone was posted was to generate tax revenue. His brief research on *Google* uncovered several instances where similar cases had been dismissed. But now his focus shifted from his traffic court hearing to this woman. He chastised himself for not wearing the charcoal black pinstripe; it was his favorite. He could feel the heat begin to rise under his crisp four-hundred-count Egyptian cotton, button-down-collared shirt. Beads of sweat started to pool just above his temples as he evaluated his appearance and began formulating a plan on how he should make his formal first impression. Past experience had proved time and time again that there was only one first meeting, and that first formal, face-to-face introduction was beyond important. Preparing for that moment, one had to do everything within one's power to maximize the encounter. He knew that today wouldn't be that day. This woman was worthy of a full-court press.

After tucking the crumpled traffic ticket back into his wallet, then letting the wallet slide down into the inner pocket of his jacket, he began to study the woman. Her long, straight black hair hung down the length of her back. She wore a pleated black wool skirt and a white silk blouse, and she sat at attention in the plastic-coated armchair designed for handling the weight of a three-hundred-pound person, not for comfort. The years of business dealings overseas paid dividends. He had acquired the ability to use his peripheral vision. It had been years since he'd been caught sneaking a peak.

In that moment, Jonathan made a conscientious effort to remain out of the woman's direct view and slid his shoulder forward, pivoting away from her view. With calculated sidesteps, he meandered away until he could walk out the front double glass doors. He decided to pay the ticket. No need for a hearing. Once inside his car, he waited as previously parked cars vacated their spots. He would reposition his car into those now vacated parking spaces. After several moves, Jonathan had strategically parked his car in full view of the front doors. Hiding behind his dark sunglasses, he waited. Exactly one hour and fifty eight minutes later, the woman exited the building.

With each step she took, Jonathan's pulse quickened. For a brief moment, he was afraid she knew what he was up to. Pushing past any sense of guilt, he depressed his cell phone camera and began recording. Only later would he replay that tape in high definition. She walked directly in front of his car. He tilted the phone angling it into the side mirror. As she approached her white *Toyota Camry*, he zoomed in, preserving her image as she depressed the remote car key. He heard the high-pitched chirp of the door locks being released. Jonathan repositioned the phone and zoomed in on her license plate.

Jonathan followed her out of the parking lot. After several miles of surface streets, she parked outside a restaurant. He continued recording her as she walked through the front doors. From the protection of his car, he watched as she tied an apron around her thin waist. He couldn't help but notice how the other workers looked at her and began busying themselves in her presence. Pulling out a paper tablet from his breast shirt pocket, he jotted down the name and address of the restaurant.

Driving back to his office, Jonathan began a mental list of things he needed. The first order of business was to complete a full identity check. As he depressed the speed dial on his cellphone, he noticed a large net from a driving range towering over the trees. Cranking his steering wheel, he turned into the parking lot, maneuvering his car into a safe isolated spot, well out of range of any errant hits. He didn't want a golf ball denting his car. With his cellphone pinched between his upper shoulder and right ear, he struggled as he yanked his golf bag out of the trunk. While walking across the pavement, he completed a call to his secretary, scheduling an appointment for next week. Even though nothing was truly set, Jonathan was being optimistic that something would happen by then. He was certain the woman wasn't Japanese. He told his secretary to schedule a meeting, allotting a three-hour window the following Tuesday afternoon. He tucked his cell phone into his golf bag and walked across the black asphalt. Approaching the ball dispenser, his mind switched gears.

Jonathan grabbed one of the tokens from the pouch in his bag. It was full of tokens so he could go straight out, not having to go to the cashier first. As he fed the coin into the automated golf ball dispenser, he watched a stream of driving range balls fall into the yellow jumbo basket from the opening below. He forced the memory of the Asian woman to the back of his mind. He needed to concentrate on the company golf tournament at Monterey. The nine best scores from each division would qualify. At present, he was ranked seventh in his division. With only one more tournament to qualify, he was confident that his best score of 79 would hold up. In either case, he could drop two positions and still qualify.

\*     \*     \*     \*     \*

Hye-Jin pulled the large bills out of the till. Her restaurant had learned from the school of hard knocks the lesson on handling cash from a prior armed robbery. From that day forward, after each peak period, lunch and dinner, they moved the large bills to the back office, keeping only enough cash in the till to make change. Walking back to the office, she thought back to the large man she had seen at the DMV. There was something about him.

As she shut the office door behind her, the bright red box of fortune cookies caught her attention. She couldn't help but laugh to herself. Many Americans had no concept of the different Asian cultures. Chinese, Japanese, Korean, Thai, Filipino, Taiwanese, Vietnamese, Cambodian—they were all the same. It surprised her how many times a week one of her customers would ask, "where are the fortune cookies?" She had long since tired of explaining that fortune cookies were a treat offered at Chinese restaurants. Inevitably, such conversations would lead her to wonder about the wisdom of explaining the fact that fortune cookies were an Americanized tradition; they had not originated from anywhere in the Orient. After much thought, she resolved herself to having the cookies available for those customers who asked.

Years before, when she had first purchased the fortune cookies, out of curiosity Hye-Jin opened three packets. To her surprise, inside were little written notes. One of those notes had a message that struck a chord. It reminded her of her grandfather. She had kept that small note taped on the wall of her office, just under the traditional first dollar bill earned that she had framed. She was told that keeping a paper dollar bill was an American tradition for good luck. Anyone who knew any Asians knew that they were all about being lucky. The fortune cookie message read: "It is inevitable that one must learn life's lessons. Otherwise, one may be forced to relive those experiences over and over again." As she placed the money into the merchant bank deposit bag, she thought back to her grandfather.

\*   \*   \*   \*   \*

"Don't ponder things that have no consequence to your life," scolded her grandfather. "Spend your energy developing your inner self. Chasing temporary selfish goals in pursuit of material wealth is not the answer."

"That's easy for you to say, Grandfather. You are already rich," replied Hye-Jin. With her head downturned, a sense of shame and embarrassment flooded over her at being chastised by her grandfather.

Watching his beautiful granddaughter looking down and avoiding eye contact, her grandfather couldn't help but smile. He was filled with love and admiration. Like many Koreans, he had been too strict with his own children. Being given a second chance with a grandchild, like most grandparents he contemplated the way he had raised his own children. Being an inexperienced parent, he still wanted to pursue his own personal ambitions. But this created a situation that blurred his judgment as a parent. Were the restrictions he placed on his children an attempt to help in their development, or did it have more to do with his pursuit of personal goals as an individual? As one gets older, he thought, one begins to come to grips with this balance between parent and self. With age, one tends to be more honest toward oneself, more capable of acknowledging one's true motivation.

As his young four-year-old granddaughter glanced up, peeking out from under her straight, jet-black bangs and evaluating whether her grandfather was still upset, he began laughing. Breaking into an ear-to-ear grin smile, he bent down and picked her up.

"That's okay! You may keep the pearls you've found, my little princess." His granddaughter's face lit up with joy and satisfaction. Rather than focusing on her writing lessons, she had sneaked out of the house to open the clams from one of his clam bins. Her grandfather owned a modest seafood market just in front of his home. As he carried her back into the house, she stretched her little hand out over his neck to grab a flower from the hanging pot overhead. He grew *Country Jasmines* year round. They were his favorite; there was something powerful about them. It was as if the flower's essence enhanced all of one's senses, like it provided an added boost of confidence.

Every morning, her grandfather would place one of the pots filled with *Country Jasmines* in the center of their table, like a living centerpiece to enjoy with their morning meals. The flowers had a unique aroma, one that she forever associated with her grandfather. When he was present, the love he showered on her created a sense of comfort and safety. She never forgot him. Just smelling that flower brought back the memory of him and that wonderful feeling that his memory instilled. But those flowers were to be handled with caution. Like many flowers, if eaten they could make a person sick. In some situations, depending on the quantity ingested, they could be lethal. Her grandfather had warned her never to eat local honey when these flowers were in full bloom. He always cared for her and referred to her as his little princess. She felt like one too.

# 6

After practicing at the driving range, Jonathan drove the long way home. Taking the 110 north to downtown LA, he would exit 4th Street and cut through downtown, zig-zagging on the surface streets and using alleys to cut back through the garment district and past *Staples Center.* After traveling through a gauntlet of stoplights, he veered off the main boulevard that ran adjacent to the now-industrialized section. Following the street down a hill, he entered his old stomping ground, a far cry from his current home in Brentwood. He made a quick stop at the *7-Eleven* to get some snacks before turning into the park. Maneuvering his *Mercedes* onto the gravel parking lot, he parked the car facing the baseball diamond.

During the summer, it had become his ritual. Every Wednesday night, he would come to this same spot and watch the boys playing Little League baseball. He didn't know any of the kids. He didn't know any of the parents. But it was a place that brought him comfort. It was something he did to remind himself of where he had come from, what he had achieved, and what he still had to look forward to.

\*　\*　\*　\*　\*

Looking out at their sons playing baseball on the field, the parents' attention was distracted as they heard gravel crunching under the weight of a car turning into the parking lot. Some parents turned their attention toward the noise. It was a new black *Mercedes* sedan.

"It's that guy again," said one of the mothers.

"Yeah, it's him. Wonder why he comes here," said another mother.

Looking at the parking lot, some of the fathers turned their attention away from the game and stared at the black *Mercedes*.

"It is kind of peculiar, right?" offered one of the fathers. "He never gets out of the car to come to the grandstand, he never goes to the restroom. Heck, he never even buys food at the concession stand. He just stays there until the end of the game." More parents turned toward the car.

"Aw, don't worry about him. He's harmless, probably just a lonely man. Maybe he's divorced and can't see his kid 'cause the ex moved away or something," suggested another father.

"Well, it gives me the creeps," offered one of the mothers.

As the inning ended and the children began coming off the field toward the dugout, the hands clapping and shouts of encouragement by the other parents brought their attention back to the game and away from the mysterious black car.

\*　\*　\*　\*　\*

Jonathan reclined his leather chair, titled the steering wheel in the full upward position and opened the glove compartment. Pulling out a large bag of salted sunflower seeds, he poured a handful and shoved a fistful into his mouth. Reaching into the back seat, he retrieved his baseball cap and pulled it onto his head. It wasn't a snap kind like he had as a child, but an all-wool fitted *Angels* cap. He hated the *Dodgers*. Pushing the salty seeds into the side of his cheek with his tongue, he lifted his large Dr. Pepper Big Gulp and took a large hit on the straw. Making sure to swallow only the liquid, no seeds, he turned his attention to the field.

As he watched the boys running out of the dugout onto the field, he felt that hollow feeling in his throat and upper chest. As the muscles in the corners of his eyes began to quiver, the memories came flooding back. Like clockwork, being there triggered his memories, and vivid images dominated his consciousness. As the first tears leaked out of his eyes, he glanced across the field over the center-field wall. In the distance, he could see the large, three-story brick building. It was still there, but now it was vacant and unoccupied. The slap against the young pitcher's glove echoed across the field as the pitcher caught the ball. The next inning was about to begin. Jonathan's childhood was spent in this one-city-block area. His fondest memories were made right here, at that same base-ball field.

*   *   *   *   *

"Hey Johnny!" smiled the Little League coach. Hearing his name, Jonathan jogged across the street to help the coach set up for that day's practice. He had been dressed for hours and was watching out the second-floor window. Sister Gladys wouldn't let him leave the building until the coach had arrived. Going to the ball field was the highlight of Jonathan's week. Those summer months were his sanctuary. That spring, he had found the courage to ask the Father for permission to join the league. He had been working odd jobs and saving his meager funds to pay for the fee.

Having sneaked out without permission to get an application from one of the coaches had been nerve wracking, something that he would never confess. He didn't want anyone to know what he had done. He had completed the application himself, using a pencil in case any changes were required. He had used his best penmanship, thinking through every question in earnest. The priest sat awestruck at how much initiative Jonathan had shown. Looking across his large wooden desk, he stared at the young boy's face. Jonathan sat frozen in the chair, holding his breath and waiting for a response. The priest understood the importance of the boy's request. Having lost both his parents to a car accident, Jonathan had come to live at The Catholic Children's Sanctuary when he was only eight years old.

He was larger than the other children, and somewhat homely and shy. It was a shame, because he was such a sweet boy. His soul was pure with a gentle temperament. Father O'Brien had always hoped that Jonathan would be adopted, but it never happened. Jonathan spent his entire childhood as one of the flock. Glancing back across the wooden desk, the Father made eye contact with little Jonathan, staring intently and waiting for his response. No child from the Sanctuary had ever been associated with Little League before. Knowing how important this decision was, Father O'Brien looked directly into his eyes and gave his blessing. He even purchased Jonathan's first baseball glove.

Like clockwork, Jonathan showed up to the practice field only minutes after the coach would arrive. It was common for Jonathan to be the first boy to arrive and the last one to leave. He treasured every minute of every practice and every game. It was as if he were surrounded by the love of the parents, able to share in the dialogue exchanged by parents and their children. It was as if he had been adopted by the twelve other families.

The coach instinctively knew that Jonathan was a special child. He never pried and never asked about his parents. Before the season had started, the coach had reviewed Jonathan's application. It included a cover letter prepared by Father O'Brien that explained the situation. Reading the information and understanding what that situation entailed was entirely different. After already beginning his drive home, the coach remembered that he had left a baseball bat in the dugout. When he doubled back and turned his car down the street toward the baseball field, he saw someone walking toward the large three-story brick building. The coach could just make out the figure of a little boy walking through the metal gate and up the large concrete steps and entering the tall, glass-windowed doors. Slowing the car as he drove by the entrance, he looked up at the building. Mounted on the side of the large brick-block walls were sizeable metal letters: "The Catholic Children's Sanctuary." It finally hit the coach, Johnny was an orphan.

# 7

"Oni, we need new menus. These are getting to look worn," said the young waitress. *Oni* is what females called each other, whether they were related or not. It meant something like *big sister*.

Examining the laminated menu, she knew that they still had several months of good use left in them, but her worker was right. They were looking a little tattered and worn. Pursing her lips and nodding her head, she acknowledged the worker's concern and set the menu back onto the table.

Shrugging her shoulders and beaming with excitement, the waitress flashed a bright smile. Being able to work for Miss Kim and being able to speak with her was a special honor. In the Korean community, Miss Kim held almost a celebrity status. As the young worker walked toward the kitchen, her cellphone began to vibrate in the back pocket of her tight denim blue jeans. Grabbing her phone, her eyes bulged with anticipation as she read the number.

"Oni, it's my man. May I take the call?" asked the young worker.

E. A. Padilla

Looking at Miss Kim, the girl looked as if she would break down in tears if she couldn't speak to her boyfriend, even though they had spoken with each other two hours before. Clutching the phone in both hands, she waited for Miss Kim's reply.

Keeping her face downturned toward her desk as if in deep concentration, she forced herself not to look up at the star-struck girl with that impressionable face. Unemotionally, she grunted "*Nay.*" ("Yes").

Bounding down the hallway to the employee lounge, the girl answered her phone and spoke with the innocent sweetness of youth—the purity of a person's first true love. The other workers couldn't help but stop what they were doing and watch her almost running to the break room. Tilting her head, Miss Kim pushed her eye glasses back to see the young lovebird almost float through the doorway. Smiling to herself, she couldn't help but be affected by the girl's positive energy— that special something that happens when a girl first falls in love. It's as if the optimism and happiness of the person in love radiates from within and somehow impacts others. Seeming to turn her attention back to the proposed coupon advertisement, Miss Kim began to recall her first true love.

*     *     *     *     *

"*Chagiya*" (Honey), "do you have to study tonight? Let's go out for some black noodles."

She had met Tae Young in her freshman history class. Seeing him for the first time left a lasting impression. He seemed perfect. He was smart, gentle, and unlike most of the other boys. She first saw him at the bookstore. He had been looking for the same history book. He had helped her locate it among the countless piles. She felt so overwhelmed, doing everything on her own. It wasn't anything like high school. College was intimidating.

As she grew up, her parents planted the vision that she would someday attend Seoul University. As a child, she would

59

be reminded by her parents that once she finished her education, she would help expand their family business. What once was a single small, family-owned local fish market had blossomed and expanded into ten separate storefronts throughout Seoul, Busan, and Jeju Island. The Kim's had become wealthy and privileged. As owner of four homes and several apartment complexes, her family followed the trend to look for a suitable match for their daughter. After countless formal dinner meetings with potential suitors, they had selected her future husband. Unlike in America, it was a Korean tradition for the parents of the well-to-do to arrange their children's marriages. Marriage was more about the family status and the strengthening of two families, and not about physical attractions and romance. It was understood that those feelings of love would develop over time. Most elderly Koreans hold the notion that emotional love is a fleeting occurrence, something that melts away as time passes. Emotional love is something that lingers for only a few years, after which life took its toll, bringing the newly-weds back down to earth to face the realities of day-to-day life. Her parents believed that love was a way to describe loyalty and perseverance. In their mind, love was the internal feeling behind each individual's decision to remain committed to a common goal, to remain faithful and present through the trials and tribulations of life. It was this decision to remain by a partner's side that defined love. Those glorified ideas depicted in the movies—holding hands, the romance, the melodramatic kisses—that wasn't real life. Such outward signs of affection were an American ideal, most definitely not a Korean one. At least, that's what she had been taught. But that all changed when she met Tae Young.

Most of the boys she had met were nonverbal, aggressive, and domineering. They had an almost militaristic attitude about life and had no personal attributes conducive to a successful marriage other than familial wealth, support, and the ultimate fear of disappointing their families. It wouldn't be love that kept a marriage together. Amongst her girlfriends, they each secretly shared dreams of romance and love. However, they too had been betrothed through arranged marriages.

Recognizing and appreciating the sacrifice her parents made, she couldn't help but feel obligated to support her parents' decisions and follow the advice and plans they had laid out for her life. She had been a dutiful child honoring the wishes of her parents, but this changed after she had met Tae Young. She now felt that there was more to life than just honoring the family and self-sacrifice for the betterment of the family. She had a life, her own life, and she wanted to experience true love, a love that centered on emotions and passion, not a love that was conceived by two sets of parents before the couple had even met.

It wasn't uncommon for a young woman from a traditional Korean business family to have never kissed a man, let alone had sex before attending the university. The Korean culture wasn't about outward signs of affection. Korean married couples seldom, if ever, kissed in public. Consequently, holding hands for her was a big deal. She remembered the first time she held Tae Young's hand as they entered the movie house. The typical Korean movie theatre looked more like the first class section on a 747 jet, with the oversized, leather-covered reclining chairs. She couldn't remember the movie that played, but she recalled the warmth from his strong hand. It was like an electric blanket wrapped around her small fingers interlaced between his. As they walked back to her dormitory room, they stopped by the koi pond. Sitting together holding hands, they looked up into the stars. She had felt so happy and safe. He was so nice and caring. Looking into her eyes, he asked for her permission before leaning toward her and pressing his lips toward her soft smile. She held her breath, closed her eyes and held her lips against his. Feeling his whisker stubble against her soft cheek, she slowly tilted her head back and enjoyed the experience of her first kiss. Slowly, their lips separated. She leaned her head against his strong shoulder and could feel the cool breeze against her face as she opened her eyes to see the bright night stars. As the steam from their breath drifted upward into the cold evening, they remained seated on the wooden bench, gazing at the star-filled sky. She would never forget that kiss, her first kiss, her first true love.

\* \* \* \* \*

Hye-Jin was an art major and an accomplished painter. At the university, she was exposed to other art forms—pencil, ink, watercolor, and sculpting—as well as the history of the great artists from the past. She had thought Art History would be an easy course. That was before she considered what a person would be tested on. At least with typical World History courses, there was a basic foundation from which one could start, something that everyone knew something about. But Art History was more like a foreign language. The tests involved viewing a slide picture and then identifying the style, time period, artist's name, title of the piece, the name of the museum where it was located, and the significance the piece had in terms of its influence on the world of art. A typical Art History final would require the student to master over 5,000 facts.

As each semester passed, Hye-Jin could feel her inner self continue to question the wisdom of accepting the arranged marriage. She continued to see Tae Young while still maintaining her dutiful obligatory visits to her betrothed family. During those visits, it was as if neither family cared that the children knew very little about each other. Neither set of parents considered their children's feelings. No one even considered that either of the young adults would object. All four parents had met their own spouses in this way. So did their parents, and their grandparents.

Given that the marriage arrangement had been reached during the first year at the children's middle school, the annual comingled family ceremonies had created a false sense of commitment nurtured by both sides. Hye-Jin had never verbalized any prior dissatisfaction about the arrangement. It was assumed by both families that the marriage was a foregone conclusion. They were wrong.

Hye-Jin's university education had taught her to peel back the onion and ask questions. Science and logic both started from a premise, an idea, a hypothesis about something. Through reason, supported by facts, followed by a thoughtful analysis of the pros and cons of a situation, students were taught to reach their own unique individual conclusion. Not all conclusions were deemed correct or incorrect. Rather, one's conclusion required proper reasoning to justify the position. As Hye-Jin continued her education at the university, the pink elephant in the room became bigger and bigger, until it could no longer be ignored. All of the skills of logic and reasoning had come full circle. Hye-Jin began asking herself why she should accept an arranged marriage. And so it started.

*    *    *    *    *

"Hye-Jin, you and Tae Young make a great couple," her room-mate yelled across their bathroom toward Hye-Jin, who was sitting alone on the living room sofa.

Looking away from the television, she stared back at her roommate.

"You know we're just friends. That's all we can be. You know that," replied Hye-Jin. Squeezing the plastic coke bottle as she tilted it up to her lips to take a drink, she contemplated her dilemma. After setting the bottle down on the end table, from frustration her index finger punished the television remote control as she started changing the channel. Even the sweet commercial with talking puppies couldn't remove the frown that began to settle across her face. It was her last year before graduation, her last year at the university, her last year with Tae Young.

Poking her head out through the bathroom door, with a hair iron stuck in her hand, her roommate stared at Hye-Jin. With the honesty that only a best friend would dare express, she said, "You're not just friends. I know you, Hye-Jin. I see you together. You two are a couple." Staring at the side of Hye-Jin's head, she began tapping her slipper-covered foot, waiting for a reply.

With squinted eyes and a quick jerk of her head, like the hem of a long skirt, Hye-Jin's hair floated across her forehead. *"Paboya!"* ("You're stupid!") was her only reply. Continuing to face her roommate, Hye-Jin rolled her eyes back toward the television. For dramatic effect, she held the remote control out in front of her eyes and with her other hand she pointed her finger into the air like someone trying to hail a taxi cab on a busy street, before dropping her hand down toward the remote control directing her anger at the channel selector. Without stopping to view what was being shown on each channel, Hye-Jin flipped through countless channels before jerking her head back toward the television, allowing her bangs to fly back in the opposite direction and sighed.

Thinking about what was said, her roommate stopped tapping her foot and ducked back into the bathroom. Under her breath, she replied, "Well, you do." She didn't realize that Hye-Jin could hear her. With a shrug of her shoulders and a deep exhale, Hye-Jin turned off the television. The abrupt loss of the volume had a quieting effect on the room. Hye-Jin looked at the blank screen and replied in soft muffled voice, "I know we do."

# 8

Jonathan stopped by the restaurant and waited, seated in his assigned booth. He had timed his visit to miss the lunch rush. He wanted a chance to meet the woman face to face. He had already done his homework and knew what he would order: *mandu* soup and barbequed short ribs called *kalbi*. He was already proficient with chopsticks. As he sat waiting for his main dish to arrive, he snacked on the multiple small hors d'oeuvres served in small round dishes with different vegetables known as *pan chan*. He noticed a newspaper article that had been replicated, framed, and mounted on the wall adjacent to each booth.

Jonathan had already read the article on the Internet. He was impressed. Although he hadn't known any Koreans, he imagined that his experience with his Japanese Company gave him an idea of what to expect. He heard a back door open and saw the woman. She was focused on reading something and didn't notice him waiting. He took advantage of her distraction and studied her appearance. He had spent so much time researching Hye-Jin that he felt like he already knew her.

Having a gift for languages, Jonathan had already started a crash course learning Korean. He had purchased a CD on *Amazon* called *In-Flight Korean*. It was a language course intended for business executives who needed to know basic verbal communication skills in an abbreviated set of lessons. The company offered the same style of course in numerous other languages. It was marketed as principally an audio course that taught a person basic skills intended to be listened to during the long flight to that country. It worked. The course didn't attempt to teach the student all of the subtle differences of a language; instead, it focused on real world, conversational words based on the most honorific respectful form of the language. This way, if the student learned the words in this manner, they were unlikely to accidentally offend someone during an ordinary conversation.

As the server approached Jonathan, he jumped right in with his new language skills and spoke. *"Annyong haseyo? Mannaso pangopsumnida."*

The young woman looked up from her notepad and glanced down at Jonathan. She couldn't help but smile as she replied "Wow, hello. It's nice to meet you too." She stepped back, placed her hand on her hip, and studied the man. From past experience, she had come to understand that some military personnel who had the benefit of being stationed in Korea had picked up the language. But in those cases, they did so without understanding the important distinctions when speaking formally or toward another person with respect. Unknown to Jonathan, the CD had taught him the formal honorific phrasing. As such, his words were not only pronounced perfectly, but were phrased with honor and respect.

"Where did you learn to speak Korean?" asked the server. She assumed it wasn't from being stationed in the military.

"I've been teaching myself. *Hangungmal chogum ahmnida,*" he replied.

"No, you speak very well," she replied.

Jonathan felt good about himself. He thought his Korean was getting better. He had been listening to the CD every time he drove and had downloaded it onto his MP Player. He listened to it when he worked out and while riding the stationary bike at the gym. Unlike a 16-hour flight, Jonathan had already put in over 50 hours of listening and parroting the phrases. Given his already high-level understanding of conversational Japanese, he thought it was easier for him to pick up his third language, Korean. It seemed easier for him to associate an object, idea, or phrase, as he had learned this skill when speaking Japanese. His mind had become accustomed to speaking in a foreign language. Making that mental shift was easier for him.

The woman completed his order and walked it back to the kitchen. As she passed Hye-Jin, she mentioned their newest patron and suggested that she should drop by and visit his table. Hye-Jin looked up at Jonathan. She saw him as very tall and stout, with a bushy mustache. Most Korean women disliked facial hair, but there was something about this man. Not intimidated by his dominating physique, she noticed that there was something else present, something she detected in his eyes and facial expression. It was as if that comfortable true self, the one that most people hide under, that self-protective default expression that most people maintain, was trying to bubble out from under the façade. For a split second, a rush of deep emotions flooded her senses. She had no idea where they had come from. Those feelings were normally only assigned to people to whom one held a deep attachment and emotional attraction, feelings that took years to develop, even though she was certain she didn't know this man. It was like an emotional *déjà vu*—an eruption of feelings based on an absolute certainty toward a person. Yet she knew she had never met this man before. It was a contradiction in logic.

However, this feeling was nothing like love at first sight. These feelings had nothing to do with a physical attraction. She was neither repelled nor drawn to him physically. His appearance had no effect on her, one way or the other. What got her attention was her sense of being somehow connected to this man. As she approached him, it was as if the feeling intensified with each step she took toward him. For some reason, she knew she could believe and trust everything this man told her. It was as if he had been protecting her from harm for years, like he had already proven himself to her time and time again. There was no need to question his friendship. It was like she knew everything about his character and inner soul before even knowing his name or exchanging a single word with him.

Jonathan made direct eye contact with Hye-Jin for the first time. At least this time he would meet her under the circumstances he had planned, not some random encounter at the DMV. This time, he had the correct attire and knew what he was going to order and say; he had played it out in his mind, over and over again. As she approached his table, he watched her posture, the gait in her stride and noticed a familiar motion, a movement that somehow struck a memory. It was a flashback deep in his mind. Her movements reminded him of a vision that seemed to visit him only in his dreams, where he never saw a face but recognized a specific walk, her body position, a cadence in her stride, a silhouette. At that moment, Jonathan froze. All of his preplanning evaporated, and his consciousness was unprepared with a flood of emotions and unexpected feelings. It was like he was being reunited with a long lost friend, rekindling a friendship that had the depth beyond an association or acquaintanceship—more even than matrimony or family. It was like encountering a soul mate, a relationship that remained intact beyond a lifetime and transcended lives. It was a strong bond that would continue throughout eternity.

As they both stared at each other without speaking, their souls seemed to embrace their essence, their space. It wasn't like they felt an uncontrollable passion as they looked into each other's eyes. It was more like they recognized the energy their souls were exchanging as they reacquainted themselves with each other. As the seconds passed, they came back to the present and began what they each perceived as a reintroduction.

"I'm pleased to meet you," Hye-Jin said as she reached out her hand. As Jonathan shook it, they could each feel the electricity between them, not a physical attraction, but a real spiritual connection. Without the need for explanations or in depth recounting of their pasts, they both paused, appreciating and accepting what they each felt.

Taken by the moment, Hye-Jin sat down at his table, electing to share a meal together. The workers were shocked. She had never done this before. He was a *mi gook saram*—an American.

It was inevitable that they would exchange information about their lives. Neither was surprised to learn that they had the same birthday, a day that all Americans celebrated. They also were born in the same year, 1964. Consequently, they shared the same Chinese Astrological sign. They were both Dragons. They didn't know it then, but they shared much more. In a relaxed conversation, they continued their meal together until closing. As Jonathan finally left the restaurant, he looked back at Hye-Jin.

"I'll see you later," he spoke in a whispered voice. Hye-Jin looked up into his eyes, smiled back, and replied, "I'll see you later.

On the first Monday night of each month, Jonathan had a ritual. He had already blocked out those days on his calendar, twelve Mondays for the year. Otherwise, if he didn't, his secretary, following the company directive, would inevitably fill them with appointments. Everyone at his firm had been trained that the more one worked, the more one accomplished, which translated into more production for the company, which theoretically should result in more profits. With more profits, there were more bonuses and more promotions. It was a win-win situation for everyone. Like most Japanese-based companies, something had changed for the worse. After World War II, Japan had to literally rebuild its country. All Japanese felt a personal responsibility to do whatever they could to contribute toward its reconstruction. It became an obsession, and they devoted most of their resources and energies to that end. Even after Japan had achieved its goals, rebuilding Japan better than before, it wasn't enough. This lopsided all-in mentality prevented Japan from returning to their pre-war balance. It was as if the Japanese continued to push their culture in hopes that by demonstrating to the world their ingenuity, flaunting their prosperity, and parading their financial success through business throughout the world, they could somehow atone for their military failures and barbaric actions during their conquest of the Pacific Rim and other Asian countries. It was as if the Japanese culture remained preoccupied with hyper occupational and professional dominance, striving for literal excellence to avoid facing past atrocities. The underlying belief was that Japan would rather work itself to death than be accountable for the past actions. This trend became so wide spread in Japan that young men without any prior health issues began dropping dead for no apparent reason. The phenomenon became so common that a name was created—*karoshi*. The literal Japanese translation was death from overwork, resulting in a heart attack or stroke attributed to stress and a starvation diet.

Jonathan believed that, had Japan prevailed in World War II, no one would be asking them to justify or apologize for their actions. It was this underlying understanding about their culture that had always interested him. In his mind, it seemed that the Japanese were humbled and coerced to justify those actions, only because of their defeat. It was the fact that they were defeated and suffered a loss of face. For this reason only, the humiliation it caused the Japanese culture, is why Jonathan believed they apologized. From their point of view, it was an apology to their emperor and all of the citizens of Japan, for the shame that the defeat had created. He didn't believe that they were apologetic for what they did, nor did they feel remorse for the pain and suffering they caused others. In Jonathan's mind, had Japan won the war, none of that would have mattered. It was the defeat that caused the shame. Japan worked so hard, to prevent the Japanese from being shamed on a global scale ever again.

Jonathan left his coat and tie in his car. He had rolled up his long-sleeved shirt and wrapped the denim apron around his waist. He tied the drawstring behind his back and adjusted the upper chest-piece before ducking his big head through the upper straps. As the apron fell into place, he could feel a smile widen across his face. Jonathan had been volunteering at the soup kitchen for the homeless for the last five years. He had earned some slight seniority in the group of volunteers, but he was still junior to several others who had been helping for over twenty years.

He didn't do much. He couldn't cook, but he could clean some mean dishes. Jonathan enjoyed this small part of his life. On his own, he had purchased jumbo-sized dish gloves from an industrial supply store. For some reason, it replenished his soul to stand in line with seven other volunteers, dutifully scouring the large bowls and cooking utensils in the deep steel triple sinks at the shelter. As he aged, he wanted to pay back Father O'Brien for allowing him to participate in the local Little League. Jonathan never forgot the kindness he had received there. He was forever in their debt, grateful for the love and happiness they provided him. It was the least he could do.

As the last pots and pans were cleaned and then dried, he noticed a new recruit who was emptying the trash cans and carrying an overflowing plastic bag of garbage out toward the alley dumpster. He had an adhesive badge that displayed his name in large capital letters—REGGIE stuck to the pocket of his flannel shirt. The use of name tags had a purpose. Only veteran volunteers and a limited number of the shelter personnel knew the significance: Only parolees were assigned name tags. It was necessary, for everyone's safety. No one wanted to put the parolees into a situation that could tempt them and jeopardize their progress toward full reintroduction to society. Nor did anyone want to put others at risk. Every parolee had to be cleared by the Parole Board and the Agent assigned when being reintroduced. For obvious reasons, ninety-nine percent of the parolees assigned here had been convicted of non-violent crimes. However, on occasion, with special rare cases, a parolee who had been convicted of a violent crime was allowed into the program. Reggie was one of those cases. The fact that his name was spelled in all capital letters also had a special meaning. An all capitalized name tag meant that the parolee had committed murder. As Reggie carried the plastic garbage bag back to the alley, he didn't notice that the other volunteers kept their distance. That night, there were three other volunteers with name tags. Only Reggie's name was spelled out in capital letters.

As Reggie walked out the back door and into the alley, he saw the bright, full moon glowing above the neighboring buildings. He paused, looking up at the star-filled sky, before slinging the slippery plastic bag up over the rim of the metal container while holding the heavy metal lid open with his free hand. After depositing the garbage into the receptacle, he let go of the lid. The vibration and metallic clanking sound as the lid slammed against the thick-bottomed rectangular container echoed against the brick buildings that lined the alleyway. Hearing that noise took Reggie back to memories from his distant youth, to a time and an event that changed his life forever.

* * * * *

Reggie had just finished his first official meet with his high school JV wrestling team. His younger brother and sister were old enough for him to pursue an extracurricular sport. The matches took place only once a week. The JV Squad meets were held earlier in the evening, before those of the Varsity Squad. It would put him home at 7:00 p.m. He would have liked to stay and watch the upperclassmen, but he was grateful just to be able to participate. He had talked to his neighbors, the Nuevos, who were like his grandparents. After discussing the idea of joining the team, they had encouraged him and offered to make sure his siblings were fed the night of his wrestling matches. His practices didn't impact him too much; they pushed back his domestic duties only an hour. The Nuevos felt it was good for Reginald to become more involved with school.

He never mentioned his new after-school obligations to his mother. Once she got home from work, she would be passed out in her room from her heroin anyway. She hadn't even noticed any change in the household. She lived on microwaved burritos, light beer, and breakfast cereals. She had relegated the responsibility of feeding his younger brother and sister to Reginald years ago. She didn't even know what her kids ate. She was an addict, and the most important thing in her life was getting high and staying that way. She never wanted to go through withdrawals. She had been confined for 48 hours on two separate occasions, both for DUI arrests. Both times, she had enough drugs in her system to keep her body at bay from withdrawals. But she could feel the initial feelings start to creep into her senses. It had frightened her. She knew that going into full withdrawal would be unbearable. Those initial onset withdrawal feelings were enough. She knew she could never let that happen. The pain would be too much. She had described it as if she were dying. She wasn't exaggerating.

Her DUI arrests had taken place twenty years earlier, before she had children. She had learned a long time ago that he biggest obstacle from remaining high was to get arrested. She had arranged her life around behaviors that allowed her to be and sustain her life as an addict. She did the necessary behaviors to sustain her habit. Work was a place to make enough money to buy her drugs and avoid being arrested. Because she had children, she had to invest some of her income to pay for their upkeep, just enough so she wouldn't bring legal attention to herself. So supporting her kids made sense. No social workers nosing around meant no potential law enforcement, which in turn meant better odds of avoiding being arrested. So in her mind, using some of her drug money toward the kids was a good investment. She never considered the money she spent on her kids as an act of love or out of obligation. No, that idea had never crossed her mind. It was simply a good decision. It increased the likelihood that she could remain in her world and remain a functioning addict. Altering that balance could jeopardize everything.

At a very early age, Reggie had taken on the responsibility of caring for his younger brother and baby sister. He had never met his father, but his next door neighbors had taken him under their wings and provided positive role models for young Reginald Chambers. Thanks to Mr. Nuevo's influence, most of his teachers had never guessed the kind of home life he was leading. The Nuevos had not been blessed with children of their own, and they taught Reggie most of his social skills. He was also exposed to typical male things such as cars, tools, and establishing self-worth. Mr. and Mrs. Nuevo never judged his mother and never criticized her obvious neglect and failure as a parent. The Nuevos were the solid figures in his life and allowed Reggie to develop a strong, good-natured attitude, encouraging him to be a positive role model for his siblings. The Nuevos taught Reggie to cook, to do laundry. They had helped him develop a good routine, a consistent set of behaviors that kept him busy and engaged with the well-being of his family, avoiding trouble that most unsupervised poor children face. They helped him with his homework, and he was able to maintain good grades throughout school.

It was a miracle that Mrs. Chambers could hold down a job, but she did. She had enough decency to pull $100 a week in cash and give it to Reggie. With that budget, he was in charge of all the meals and household items. Mrs. Chambers worked at a local check-cashing store downtown. She had lost her license to drive due to multiple DUI convictions. It was a Godsend, as they didn't have to worry about the expenses associated with a car. They all walked wherever they went. The only bill she had to worry about was rent and utilities. Her boss owned their rental house. Because the check-cashing business also included the collection of utility bills, her boss deducted her rent and utilities from her pay. She never had the responsibility or burden of floating those bills. The owner knew she was an addict, but he understood her situation. She needed her job for the drugs, and everyone understood her limitations. She answered phones and processed utility payments. She could never be trusted with the cash and would defer all cash transactions to the owner.

Reggie watched a passing car as he waited to cross the street. His legs were sore from his wrestling match. He loved wrestling. He didn't understand until years later that wrestling allowed him a way to release some of his anger: the anger he felt against his mother, for her lack of emotional involvement with their lives; for the frustration of being from a single-parent family; for being poor; for having to take care of his siblings while his mother and God-only-knew-who-else lay in her bedroom passed out high on heroin. But those feelings he buried deep down, so deep that he never even knew they existed. The fact was, Reggie loved his younger brother and sister. They depended on him for everything. He could feel their eyes yearning to see him as he walked through the front door each evening, as they ran to his side, eager to share their day with him. They loved him so deeply and understood how important he was to their survival.

Reggie was a sensitive, smart young man, a survivor; one of those special people who could overcome any adversity. The Nuevos provided him with the confidence, encouragement, and support to keep his little family pushing forward, surviving in their most difficult and fragile situation. His selfless devotion to his siblings was what motivated him. He remained the key in the cog that kept that wheel turning. His discovery of wrestling gave him a constructive, organized, and appropriate way to channel all the underlying emotions he had kept bottled up deep in the recesses of his psyche—so deep that he didn't even know they existed.

Reggie jogged across the asphalt roadway in front of his house. He could feel the ache in his thigh and calf muscles from his earlier match and stepped up onto the curb. Twisting the duffle bag strap up onto his shoulder, he rubbed his bicep muscle. The soreness in his muscles brought a smile to his face.

After weeks of practicing his head and arm choke hold, he had finally mastered the move, using it that night to win his first official match. He was now 1–0 for the year and had visions of making the varsity squad next year. He could sense that he was good at this sport. During practices, he could tell by the looks he received from his wrestling partners that they were somewhat intimidated. He was right. Everyone on the team recognized Reggie's talent. Not only was he quick and immensely strong, but he also had the work ethic and physical stamina that only other athletes could appreciate. Although he was quiet, he wasn't afraid. Neither did he feel like he had anything to prove. He was far from a showoff. Reggie's daily struggle through life created an inner fire that constantly burned. He held a competitive advantage in terms of surviving life. He had a special inner spirit that, though hidden from sight, was always available and ready to ignite at any moment. It was like an untapped energy source just beneath the surface, barely in control and without limits, ready to come flooding out. As Reggie focused and learned more moves, improving his skill set, it was obvious to everyone that he was unstoppable. He was a bomb, ready to explode.

It was a strange situation. They all benefited from their little arrangement. They were so fortunate to have the correct people in their lives: The owner of the check-cashing store for giving Mrs. Chambers the opportunity, her financial arrangement that prevented her from getting money she couldn't control, and having the Nuevos as neighbors who looked out after little Reginald, who it turn took care of his siblings. It was a perfect set of circumstances. This unique arrangement kept the fragile Chambers family surviving. It was a perfect storm, an unusual balance that worked. But that all changed one day in the fall, near Reggie's sixteenth birthday.

# 9

As he made his way to the cafeteria for lunch, the intern folded the paperwork that HR had given him and stuffed them into his pocket. The morning had passed by without fanfare. He was excited about the internship and had promised himself he would gain as much experience as he could from this opportunity. Until now, everything he knew about psychology he had learned through lectures and books. Other than the unofficial psychoanalysis he performed on his family and friends, he had no practical real-life experience. This internship would give him the important hands-on experience he had been yearning for. He needed some means to help him determine if he had chosen his correct career path. He was certain that this experience would help him make the right choice.

As he walked by Hye-Jin's art studio, he smelled the strong sweet aroma, one that he had become accustomed to since his birth. In his home town, his parents' longtime neighbors had been amateur florists of some sort, having a diverse and large greenhouse on their property. Upon his birth, they had given his parents a potted flowering plant that had come from their homeland between Korea and China. It was unique and special. The isolation of this sub-mountainous region allowed a hybrid of the Rose of Sharon, the country's national flower, and a variety of Azalea and *Gelsemium elegans*. This natural phenomenon was unique to this part of Asia, resulting in a flower petal that exhibited stunning colors combined with the release of a sweet perfume that added to its unique quality. The flower had come to be known as *Country Jasmines* by the locals. The simple gift from his neighbors had become a constant part of his family's décor. His neighbors had continued to share that plant with his family throughout his entire life, bringing it by for every special occasion or celebration. The flowers were never cut from the plant. The entire plant had been given to them. As a result, Greg's parents decided to create their own small flower garden. As time passed, the Offord's had several rows of *Country Jasmines* with varying different colors. The rose garden had been planted just outside of his bedroom window. He had smelled them every day since the day he was born until the day he left home to attend college. Smelling that aroma now caused his mind to reconnect with feelings and emotions associated with family, home, and comfort.

Glancing through the open door, Greg paused, staring into the room. Sitting on the nightstand next to the thick, institutional-grade, screened-in open window was a bouquet of his favorite flower. The cool breeze sent the sweet aroma drifting through the stale, enclosed confines of the mental ward. The aroma reconnected him with the emotions associated with his parents' house. Without realizing it, he kept staring at the plastic vase.

Hye-Jin tiled her head up away from the canvas to peer over the top of her easel. She saw an intern with new scrubs and a shiny new ID badge staring at something inside her studio. She stood up and walked toward the open door.

"Do you know what they are?" she asked the intern. Without thinking still looking at the flowers, Greg replied, "Of course, they are *Country Jasmines*. They are my favorite." He continued, "They originated from China but are related to one of the most popular flowers in Korea—the Rose of Sharon. They were always around me when I was growing up." Breaking his gaze, Greg turned his attention to the voice and realized it was the beautiful Asian woman who had intrigued him from earlier in the morning.

Hye-Jin set her paintbrush down and walked toward the intern. "That's right. Most people don't know their origin. Do you know their unique story?" she asked.

Rolling his eyes upward, trying to access childhood memories, he did recall something his neighbors had told him. They had warned him to respect them. Even though they were beautiful, he had to be careful around them. "I can't remember exactly, but I believe that there is something dangerous about them," he replied. Pausing for a moment, Hye-Jin took a deep breath, enjoying the strong aroma of the *County Jasmines*. Listening to what the intern said, she thought of her own difficulty at remembering some things as well, and couldn't recall much about the flowers either. At present, all she knew for sure was that she enjoyed them and had arranged for her florist to deliver a fresh bouquet two times a week.

Breaking from her trance, she spoke again to the intern. "You know a lot about *Country Jasmines*."

"It's just one of those things, I guess. I've been around them all of my life," Greg replied. Flashing a small smile, the intern lost his concentration as he became more comfortable, happy and at peace. Hearing the cafeteria door as it slammed closed reminded him that his lunch break was ticking away. "You'll have to excuse me, ma'am, but I need to finish my lunch. My break time is almost up."

Hye-Jin smiled ever so slightly and bowed, bending from the waist. As she straightened her back, she thought back through vague memories, trying to recall the last time she had bowed in this fashion. She deduced that it must have occurred when she last met one of the elders at a Korean Chamber function years before. Her memories were still foggy about many issues from her past. She reasoned that the urge to bow must have been a result of discussing the flowers. Those flowers reminded her of her grandfather. Maybe she had become confused, and that's why she bowed in the presence of the intern. It didn't make sense, because he was much younger than she was. Bows of that nature were reserved for elders and people who maintained a high status in the community. Letting those thoughts run inside of her mind, Hye-Jin turned back toward the easel and began the final touches to her painting. There wasn't much time left.

As she continued painting, she thought back to some of her grandfather's many sayings. She could almost hear his voice as her thoughts began to drift back.

*　*　*　*　*

"My princess, time is precious. Time is something that should never be wasted. It can never be gotten back. We are each granted only so many hours, so many seconds. Our life is like the grains in an hourglass. Once the last piece of sand tumbles down to the bottom chamber, there are no more to follow."

"So do we all have the same amount of sand, Grandpa?" little Hye-Jin asked.

"No. We each have our own separate personalized clocks. Some people are given clocks that run a long time, while others are only able to enjoy a brief amount of time here," he answered.

"How come? That's not fair," she replied.

"As you get older, you'll see things differently. But that's why it is very important to spend your time wisely. Don't get distracted by unimportant matters. Be more impressed with people who devote their time toward people in their life. Although some items have a high materialistic value, no matter its worth, the worldly value of an item cannot compete with the most precious present a person can give another person— their time. Think about a person who chooses to spend their remaining minutes, their last grains of sand from their hourglass, with someone else. Does that make sense?" her grandfather asked.

Hye-Jin pondered her grandfather's question. It did make sense. No matter what the value of any object was worth, no matter how much an item was worth, what value could one place on the last remaining minutes of a person's life? She looked up into her grandfather's eyes and nodded her little head. "Yes, grandfather. I understand."

# 10

Jonathan was aware of another guy. He had been doing some of his own vetting and found out that Cameron had been married before. There was a mysterious fire where his wife had died. The article described the event as a tragic accident, but Jonathan thought something wasn't right. He knew that working with the Japanese company for all those years, having everyone scrutinizing each other, having to deal with recorded telephone conversations, had created a permanent bias in the way he viewed people in general. But even with this self-awareness about his skewed point of view of reality, his intuitive nature wouldn't allow him to back away. Like a starved dog gnawing on a bone, Jonathan couldn't let it go.

The weeks preceding the boat trip, he had not only been snooping around the Internet, but he had hired a private investigator to look into Cameron's background. What was discovered had shocked Jonathan. Hye-Jin's other suitor had not only been married twice before, but he had also legally changed his name. Worse yet, the investigator had discovered that his first wife had also died in an accidental overdose. The investigator also confirmed that, at one time, her husband had been considered a suspect in her death. Upon learning this information, Jonathan wanted to get a better grip on the situation, so he contacted a friend who had graduated from UC Berkeley. His friend was a statistics guru and was now working for one of the Bay Area tax firms. He had him run the numbers. Not accounting for the odds of being married, which complicate the equation, his friend confirmed that there was only one chance in 6,864 to die from an overdose in any given year in the US. Similarly, there was only a one chance in 115,580 of dying in a fire. However, the issue was more complicated than that. His friend had to then factor in the odds of a person's being married to two different people and the fact that each spouse would die, one from an accidental overdose and the other spouse later in a fire. Determining that answer caused many a sleepless night for his friend. While waiting to hear the final results of his inquiry, Jonathan began to understand the effort his friend was undertaking in an attempt to give him an accurate answer. It became clear to Jonathan that it was extremely unlikely that both of those events would occur naturally. Bottom line, it was a slim-to-none chance that those two events would happen to a person during his lifetime. Such a person probably had a better chance of winning the lottery. That fact changed everything.

Jonathan couldn't help it. He had always been a numbers guy. In his world, numbers never lied. One of his favorite quotes had come from his sales manager. "Don't tell me about the birth, just show me the baby," which translated into don't tell me about what happened, but show me the results. Jonathan looked at the folder. He had all of the printouts detailing all his research. He tucked the folder next to the picnic basket and continued to contemplate when he should bring all this up with Hye-Jin. He didn't want to ruin the outing, but at the same time he knew he had to tell her. Something deep down inside his soul screamed out for him not to delay and to warn her now. His most important priority in life right now was to protect her. As he closed the trunk lid of the car, he thought about what he wanted and selfishly decided to tell her later. He rationalized that he didn't want to ruin a perfect day. If only he had known what would happen next, it could have changed everything.

* * * * *

Something strange was happening with Cameron. He was changing. After visiting Hye-Jin and Barbara at the coffee shop, his entire life's purpose began to change. He no longer worried about accumulating more wealth. If he looked at his financial situation, his 403(b) retirement account was doing fine. He owned his house outright without a mortgage. Even the property tax rate was reasonable. When he had purchased the home, the real estate market had just bottomed out. Since then, he had never needed to refinance the home. As a result, the tax basis had never been recalculated. His taxes were based on his original purchase price, which was based on the home's lowest value over the last thirty years. Even without his hidden treasure, Cameron had achieved what most families would never achieve in the entire life. He was set.

Cameron sat on the sofa inside his empty home, and for the first time he began to feel restless and uncomfortable. As the television program he had been watching went to a commercial break, he no longer gloated over his hidden treasures above the fireplace. Those objects had somehow become reminders of his greed. And with those feelings, for the first time, he started to ask himself new questions about why his prior wives had fallen in love with him in the first place. His conscious mind began to somehow regret his actions in manipulating these women. That inner self-absorbed personality tried to knock some sense into him, but it was losing the battle. Never before had the selfish aspect of his inner nature felt compelled to step forward to justify itself and its prior actions. It just did what it did because it knew what it wanted. Previously, Cameron's narcissistic mind had never been challenged. As a consequence, it was ill equipped with the mental muscle power and pressure that the subconscious brain could produce when it wanted to flex all of its resources.

The narcissistic side of him lacked the ability to defend its pursuit of wealth. To point Cameron in the direction of a target, or encouraging him to acquire a new skill set for the pure purpose of extracting the wealth from another unsuspecting future spouse, no longer held up to rational thought. This new self-examination process that evaluated right versus wrong had, until now, never come into play. Unlike most "normal" people, Cameron hadn't faced the moral consequences of his actions simply because he was amoral, feeling no guilt. In order for a person to feel guilt, he had to care. One had to be able to empathize with another person's point of view, before one could form the concept of regret. Until now, none of those concepts had existed for Cameron. *What is happening?* he thought.

As the television commercials ended and his normal program *Forensic Files* resumed, Cameron quickly turned his upper body away from the fireplace, and his face exhibited a twisted expression of disgust and regret. Those feelings began to sink deeper into his soul as he began to realize that he no longer felt that surge of adrenaline and excitement over watching *CSI*, *Dexter,* or the movie *Fargo*. Those DVDs had been his staple. In the past, he had looked forward to his marathon binge watching of those shows. Now, they not only lost their appeal but left him with a sense of guilt, feeling like he had just been caught by his parents watching pornography. For the first time, Cameron felt guilt and regret over what he'd done, and those feelings began to fester inside and spread.

The ringing of his cellphone interrupted his self-deprecating thoughts. Just hearing the ringtone from the YouTube sensation song, *"Gangnam Style,"* he knew it was Hye-Jin calling him. As he answered the phone, his mood changed to a happy and positive one.

"Yoboseyo?" Cameron said as he pushed the green button.

"Hi, Cameron!" Hye-Jin spoke in an elevated, excited voice. "It's Hye-Jin!"

"I know it's you! That's why I answered in Korean," replied Cameron with a comical smile in his voice. He had already forgotten how he was feeling before she called.

"I really enjoyed the movie we went to last week. I appreciate you going to the Korean Theatre too. I hope the subtitles were okay?"

"No, seriously," said Cameron." I really enjoyed it. I couldn't believe how determined that Admiral was. I started researching his life. I'd never heard of him before. They say everything in the movie is true."

"Yes, it's all true. Maybe someday the story of Yee Soon Shin will be common knowledge in America, just like it is in Korea," she replied.

"Who knows; maybe." replied Cameron, as he sat up on his sofa with an ear-to-ear grin, not worrying about missing his show. In prior years, he would have never taken the call. He would have let it go to voicemail and then contemplated later if he would even listen to the message at all.

"I'm sorry for disturbing you, Cameron, but I have just been notified by the Korean Chamber of Commerce that I will be honored this year as their Business Woman of the Year. It's kind of embarrassing, but... if you wouldn't mind accompanying me to it?" Hye-Jin asked, looking shyly at her feet as she held the phone, waiting for his response.

"I'd be honored to," Cameron answered without any hesitation. "What day is it, and what's the dress code?" The excitement of her invitation caused him to stand and walk to the kitchen to check his calendar.

"It's next Saturday night at 7:00 p.m. It will last about three hours, with dinner and Korean entertainment. It's at the Beverly Hotel," Hye-Jin clarified, smiling to herself, relieved that he had accepted her invitation. "Oh, it's formal; so, yes, a tuxedo would be required."

"I'm writing it down on my calendar as we speak. This sounds great! Thank you so much for asking me, Hye-Jin. I'm super excited. *Kamsahamnida*."

"Yes, *Kamsahamnida*. Thank you so much," she replied.

"I'll pick you up at 6:30; that should give us plenty of time," he said.

"Cameron, you may be the only *mi-gook saram*, I mean American, there. Is that okay?"

"Absolutely. It will feel like when I was in Korea."

"Well then, I'll see you at 6:30. Good-bye."

As Cameron laid his cell phone onto the living room coffee table, he felt a rush, an unexpected surge of energy, a sense of anticipation. Although he'd felt these emotions before, these were different. In the past, he had only experienced them after he had determined the financial worth of one of his targets. In past times, those feelings had always been associated with objects. This time, he didn't even know Hye-Jin's net worth. Stranger yet, he hadn't even tried to gain that information. For the first time, despite having been married twice before, he recognized that money hadn't played any part in the motivation to establish this relationship. Determining what kind of relationship this would become was yet to be seen. At the very least, it could be the beginning of a sincere friendship.

The sense of newness and happiness and the forming of a friendship was all new to him. He grabbed the remote control and began channel surfing. He was not following his normal routine. As he mindlessly depressed the channel button on the remote, he paused on the Comedy Channel, one that he never watched. He kept it there to watch the full one-hour standup routine. He never even considered flipping between programs. It was like a switch had flipped in his head. Cameron was on a totally different track.

However, some bells can never be unrung. Some things in life continue to resonate, sending out ripples within the pool of life. Regardless of the changes a person undergoes, regardless of the apologies one expresses, some things are so devastating, so impactful, that no amount of effort can alter the effect created by those momentous events. It's like when a large sheet of ice calves off a glacier and plunges down into the bay; the weight and gravity of the ice collides with the once tranquil ocean water with such a force that an uncontrollable wall of water is thrust upward above sea level, creating a wave that travels outward across the sea. There is no way to reduce the chain reaction without creating another equally devastating event that could counter the energy that was created.

As with physics, life's energy, the ripple effect of our actions, is sent out into the universe. Unless some opposite force intercedes, there will be a cascading chain reaction. In Cameron's prior life, lived as Lee, he caused two very devastating monumental events that prematurely ended the natural lifespans of two innocent women. The fact was, they both lost their lives because of the greed of another person, not in an act of self-defense. No lofty goal or achievement was being pursued. The women hadn't died protecting another person. No, it was none of those reasons. They had died because Cameron had placed his wants and desires above all else. He had reduced their lives down to their literal financial net worth. Cameron, also known as Lee, had changed everything. There was no way to un-ring that bell. The great wave he had created had been rolling along for a decade now. It was just a matter of time before it came crashing down around him. He just didn't know it yet.

\* \* \* \* \*

For several months, Jonathan had set his mind on the new love of his life, Hye-Jin. The fact that she had only seen him in her restaurant was of no consequence. In his mind, she was it. In his mind, she was his.

Jonathan appreciated the fact that he had little experience with women. In fact, he was terrible when it came to love. He had spent many a sleepless night contemplating this issue. He had rightly concluded that being an orphan, and now having a career in the competitive marketing arena for a Japanese international corporation, had not been an environment that nurtured his skills in romance. Nor did it help him understand women. In Jonathan's mind, men were from Mars and women were from Venus, and he resided on Mercury. Until he had met

Hye-Jin, Jonathan had accepted this inadequacy in his skill set. Until now, establishing a long term relationship wasn't part of his game plan. Making money and distancing himself from his meager beginnings at the orphanage was his motivation.

Until now, having a girlfriend had no upside. Having a girlfriend would distract him from his job and most likely reduce his financial resources. Furthermore, depending on her temperament and actions, such a relationship could have serious negative consequences with upper management. His significant other would have to accept the expectations and demands that the corporation would place on him as their employee. Her perceived attitude could be detrimental to his career. She had to share the idea of being one-hundred-percent committed to the company, and recognize that it was the first and foremost priority in their life. It was above family, children, and a spouse. In this culture, the spouse of a young executive who had aspirations of climbing the company ladder had to understand that living the good life came only after years of sacrifice.

There was no expectation that employees would be in a position to enjoy the job during those earlier years. That type of thinking was an American concept and cultural weakness best exemplified by inferior products, receding market shares, while simultaneously balancing demanding unions that cried for more benefits and higher wages. Behind closed doors, it appeared that they despised the US workforce and its culture, only tolerating it out of necessity. Regardless of what other cultures believed, most consumer products and services were purchased and consumed by the good old US of A. As such, Jonathan's company had learned to bite its tongue and grudgingly accepted the situation. Failure to grasp this understanding was entrepreneurial suicide.

Jonathan had made a point of placing large delivery orders at Hye-Jin's restaurant for his office functions. He also ate at the restaurant at least three times a week. He attempted to stand out every time he was there so that all the workers knew his name and recognized him as one of their biggest single patrons.

Although Jonathan didn't know much about love, he knew a lot about business and human nature. He was hoping that his customer status would gain him favor with Hye-Jin. He was hoping she would be reluctant to turn down his request for a date, fearing he might be offended and lose his business. What Jonathan failed to recognize was that Hye-Jin, from the first time she had met him, had some unexplainable feelings toward him. Not necessarily romantic feelings, but deep and profound nonetheless. Unknown to Jonathan, Hye-Jin would have accepted his offer regardless.

The day of their date was approaching. All of his preparations were complete. His only disappointment was learning that she had also been on several dates with another man. At this point, it didn't appear to be too serious. They weren't exclusive yet, so Jonathan was going all out. He'd done some initial reconnaissance. His research had uncovered that the other man was a teacher by the name of Cameron Sivesind. He taught at a public high school. Jonathan had learned early in his career never to underestimate his competition.

Jonathan did what he had always done and took his research to another level and hired a private investigator. What he had uncovered, if true, was extremely dangerous. To get a better understanding about what he was up against, he started following Cameron whenever he had some extra time.

# 11

Mike had been searching on the Internet for a Cameron Sivesind in Los Angeles. He had hoped that the name was unique. The problem was that most people gave up their land lines for cell phones. And due to the overwhelming abuse by auto-dialers used by telemarketers, most people had asked for unlisted numbers or DO NOT CALL mandates to prevent receiving those annoying calls. As to the older population who kept land lines and didn't know about the DO NOT CALL lists, many of them listed only their first initial as opposed to a full name. Consequently, there were a one hundred thirty-six total potential C. Sivesind's residing in Los Angeles County. Mike turned to some street view programs on the outside chance that he could see a picture of the '67 *Ford Mustang* parked on the street or in the driveway. He was going through each address listed, starting at the top of the list. But up until now, he'd had no luck.

Mike tried other view sites, using real estate sites and of course Google Views. He tried tracking down twenty potential listings starting at the top of the search list. He wasn't making any progress. He took a snack break, making a beeline to the kitchen. After filling a large cup with ice and then topping it off with a frothy *Mug Root Beer* poured from an aluminum can, he devoured an entire bag of *Lay's* barbecue potato chips before walking back to the computer. As he sat down at the computer desk, he looked at the photograph of his sister sitting on the car and decided he would go straight to the address that Chuck had given him. It was a longshot, given that the DMV information was over ten years old. The buyer had probably moved.

As he stretched his arms and neck, Mike adjusted his ergonomically correct computer chair with rollers so he could prepare for another several hours in front of the monitor. He entered the address and checked the real estate listings that topped the search. He checked the Zillow.com listing first, no photos. He then checked the Trulia real estate listing. Jackpot! That one had street photos, and he had found the needle in the haystack: There it was, a red *Ford Mustang* parked on the street. The license plate had been blurred out but, boy, it sure looked promising! He glanced sideways away from the image on the computer screen, comparing it to the image in the photo with his sister. The rims looked the same. Mike turned his attention back to the computer.

*Now, why didn't I check that address first? I could have saved two hours.* He took a deep breath and chastised himself for being negative. There was no need to beat himself up like that; it wasn't doing any good. *Stay positive.* Mike studied the photograph. *It could be a dated street photograph from years before.* But then, questioning his reasoning, he thought, *Why am I assuming that he moved? Hmm. Now what?*

Mike looked out the side window of his apartment and contemplated his next move. *There was no Cameron Sivesind that also had a listed number with an address.* He thought through some options. He could call every listed number and just ask if they owned a '67 *Ford Mustang*. Although this would limit his search from the total names available, he would still have to make one hundred sixteen calls—not his first choice. As he contemplated that option further, he considered the fact that there would be long distance call charges and that most people would screen their calls and not pick up the call, letting the call go to their voicemail. The likelihood of that was especially high, given he was calling from an unusual area code. He could *67 the call and block his number from being shown. But that was probably worse than letting them see his area code.

He considered paying a third party service to do a basic background check on each of these people, but those fees would add up. Before he spent one penny, he wanted to weigh his options. If he started that process, he would have to follow it all the way through for fear of omitting a person from the search. He didn't want to throw away money like that. At $35 per search, that was over $4,000. There had to be a better way of finding Lee. He knew that there would be additional expenses coming when he did find Lee. He had to pay for the plane ticket, hotel, food, and rental car. As Mike pondered his next move, he wondered if there were any pictures of this Cameron Sivesind guy. Human curiosity piqued his interest. So rather than focusing on the street views, he changed his search criteria and began searching images of a Cameron Sivesind in Los Angeles and pushed the enter button. The first page results were uneventful, but when he went to the next page, there it was. The first photo on the page. There was no doubt. He did appear older, but that was a picture of Lee for sure.

Mike double clicked the link and waited for it to load. The picture that populated the screen was much larger and in high definition. There was no doubt in his mind. It was Lee Fullem, his sister's husband. Unable to comprehend what he was looking at, Mike sat frozen, staring at the screen. Below Lee's picture, there was another link. Mike clicked on that link. It took him to a newspaper article detailing an event involving Cameron Sivesind. The photograph of Lee had been used in the newspaper article. As Mike read the article, his blood pressure rose and his hand holding the computer mouse began to shake. The article described a tragic accidental fire. Mr. Sivesind's wife had died from smoke inhalation. The couple had no children. The Fire Department Cause and Origin Division had concluded that it was a faulty attic wire. It had taken place while Mr. Sivesind had been attending a faculty meeting at the Beverly Hills High School where he taught. Otherwise, he could have been killed as well.

Mike pushed away from the computer desk with such a force that he rolled backwards a great distance, all the way into the center of his small dining room area. Mike screamed at the computer monitor, his words echoing in his sparse apartment. "You bastard, you did it again!"

\*     \*     \*     \*     \*

As the custodians began clearing the cafeteria, patients began to return to their normal activities. Hye-Jin remained at her table. She watched the other tables being cleared, washed, and dried, while several custodians mopped the floor. They never rushed the patients out of the room, not unless they had become unruly or aggressive. Hye-Jin was somewhat of a celebrity and held a special place in the hearts of the workers. Her artwork was amazing, and her beauty caused others to naturally extend her respect. Hye-Jin looked at one of the custodians as he began mopping her area. She looked at him as if to ask him if she needed to leave.

"No, no, you're fine, Miss Kim. Don't let me disturb you. You're fine right there, ma'am. I can work around you, no problem" he said with a bright smile.

Hye-Jin looked back at him with a soft controlled smile and remained seated. Toward the back of the room one of the other custodians shouted out, "Don't be interrupting the princess. She's tending to her courtyard." The other custodians looked up, glanced around the room, and noticed that all the patients had left except for Hye-Jin. Exchanging looks, many of the custodians laughed.

"Never mind those guys, Miss Kim. You are a princess, a real nice woman. Never mind them," he offered her in a sympathetic tone, and continued mopping.

Hye-Jin didn't understand the meaning of their laughter. She returned his smile and remained seated, thinking back to her grandfather. Whispering to herself, she said, "Princess. My grandfather used to call me that... Princess." And she became lost in her thoughts.

*     *     *     *     *

It had been several weeks since her accident in the canoe. Hye-Jin had almost drowned when she had waited for her father's return. He was only steps away when a large wake caused by a passing ferryboat had capsized the canoe. She was dumped into the cold morning river water. Ever since that event, she was unable to venture back into the boat. She even had difficulty with bathing and visiting the communal saunas. Her grandfather sat her down, hoping to help her regain her confidence.

"Now, Princess, you must remember, your parents and I would never let anything happen to you. We have been given the privilege of watching over you and protecting you from harm. In life, each of us is protected. And being a protector is the most important job that parents and grandparents are tasked with in this life. The privilege of children comes with the responsibility of looking after them and protecting them. If we do our best, if we forsake our own selfish needs in pursuit of what's best for everyone in our family, we may be granted the greatest gift—to remain attached together throughout eternity."

He bent down and cradled her small face in both of his hands. Leaning forward so his eyes were in direct line with and separated from hers only by inches, he continued. "If we do that, we may have the great joy and opportunity to remain connected and the possibility of being reconnected into our next life. So you see, my Princess, your parents and I, we would never do anything to hurt you. Our love for you is genuine. You are special. You're going to make a difference in this world. I have so much I want to share with you."

As Hye-Jin recalled her grandfather's words, she recognized that at the time he had spoken those words, she didn't understand their meaning. But from his tone and facial expressions, even as a very young child, she felt his love and kindness. At that time, she didn't need to understand the words. The human brain could do some amazing things. In this case, it had cataloged those conversations, those specific memories, and replayed them verbatim at a time when their literal meaning could be understood. Hye-Jin continued to let the memories of her grandfather play out in her mind.

"Princess, even though your parents and I are here now, there will be a time when we will go on to the next stage of our lives. When that happens, I promise you, there will always be others who will come into your life, to provide you with the guidance and protection you need. You may not recognize them at first. It may take some time. But, eventually, you will understand what is happening. There will be a deep connection with these people, as if you've known each other your entire lives. There will be no doubt. You will know. You will have a calm sense of certainty."

"You must remember." He paused and leaned even closer to her, almost nose to nose, and continued speaking. "Life is a privilege. It is no guarantee. Throughout our life, we must each decide our own path. Being honest and never being involved with the taking of another human life, even our own. To do otherwise will certainly alter your spiritual endeavors. To do so, you most assuredly will have to come back. As what, no one knows. My Princess, avoid this at all costs. Otherwise, we may be separated. Anyone of us could be isolated from the other, never to see each other again, for eternity. This is our destiny."

As Hye-Jin replayed those words, she knew that she was remembering them perfectly. She recalled her grandfather's retelling her the same thing hundreds of times. Every occasion they were alone together, he repeated the same message. It was as if he wanted to make sure that she had this information hardwired into her psyche. Like the Pacific Islander tradition where an elder has a young child recite its birth lineage to permanently engrain that historical catalog. Like the book of *Matthew Chapter 1*, where there is a recounting of a genealogy from Abraham to Joseph and Mary. In a similar way, this was her grandfather's way of passing down information he believed to be vital to her life. But why? Why was it so important?

Hye-Jin heard a loud noise. It was the closing of the solid wood cafeteria doors that broke her trance. She blinked her eyes and expelled a deep breath. As her eyes focused, she scanned the room. It was empty. She was alone. As a courtesy, the custodians had left the light on. She stood from her table and glanced up at the caged clock hung high up the cafeteria wall. It was 2:45 p.m.

\*   \*   \*   \*   \*

Mike sat at his kitchen table. He had ordered a large pepperoni pizza. In a daze, he grabbed the last slice—it was cold and stiff. He bit down on the leathery food and chewed while staring at the stack of printouts that now covered his kitchen table. Those papers contained all the information he had gathered about Lee Fullem, now known as Cameron Sivesind. Everything he needed to know he found over the Internet. The last article he had printed had a picture of Lee with a beautiful Asian woman named Hye-Jin Kim, also from Los Angeles. It was a wedding announcement detailing their engagement. The wedding date was to be the weekend before the Fourth of July. Mike contemplated the timeframe. He had only fourteen days before the wedding to do something.

He couldn't prove anything. All he knew was what his gut told him. If he didn't do something, another unsuspecting woman would die from some accident. He was sure of it. But Mike didn't know what to do. He had no real game plan. All he knew was he had to get to LA. He changed the search on his computer and began looking for airline reservations. After checking the cost of several different airlines, he pulled out his credit card, completed the purchase online and sat waiting for his email confirmation. The loud "ding" echoed out of the computer's external speakers. He switched tabs, opened his Gmail account, and read the confirmation information. It was nonstop from Lincoln, Nebraska, to *LAX*, departing on the weekend.

As he printed the open-ended ticket, he made a mental note to put in for his vacation. It wouldn't be a problem. He had already carried over three weeks of vacation time from last year. Management had been bugging him for months to take some time off. He was already at the maximum carryover limit. It was either use it or lose it. He knew time off from work was a done deal.

As he started to contemplate his finances, he first thought of his credit card. Other than the airline ticket that he had just purchased, it had a zero balance with a $20,000 credit limit. He hadn't done anything for the last ten years that warranted any extra spending. He just paid rent, utilities, food, and insurance—that was it. No girlfriend and no hobbies, and this meager apartment he had been living in since he had moved out on his own. He was far from rich, but he had the time and financial means to take this impromptu vacation.

Mike went back online and made a rental car reservation. Then he started looking for hotels. He knew that after landing in LA, he would need to stay at least seven days, maybe more. This timeframe would put him in LA up until and possibly through the scheduled wedding date. He had to decide what to say to the woman. *I have to do something*, he thought.

Mike closed the computer search windows and looked at the calendar he had tacked onto the wall in his kitchen. It had been years since Mike had felt a sense of purpose. At that very moment, he wasn't happy, but he wasn't depressed either. He felt motivated. As he stood and walked back to his bedroom, he glanced back at the photograph of Annalisa. This time, he now felt a sense of accomplishment, a sense of perseverance. He hadn't given up. He had been right all this time.

He studied his sister's image in the photo, and she appeared to have a slight smile, almost as if expressing her thanks for his persistence. He had never given up. He was the only one who had figured it out. His hunches had been correct. If she could talk to him, she would tell him how proud she was of him. If she could reach out and touch him, she would. It was like her energy, her essence, was still present, trapped in this earthly plane. Her time had not been used up. She still had grains of sand in her hourglass to use. If she could somehow interact with him, she would give him a huge hug and kiss on his forehead. It was as if that picture had helped guide her brother to this exact point. It was destiny.

Mike picked up the framed photograph and kissed the glass directly over his sister's face, before turning and walking toward his bedroom. He had never felt more powerful than at that very moment in his life. Still fully dressed, he kicked his shoes off before crawling into his bed and thinking *It won't be long now.* Within minutes he fell into a deep sleep, the best night's sleep he'd had in years.

# 12

Greg Offord, the intern was coming back from his tour in the billing department. He was so glad he wasn't going to be doing that job. Coordinating the bills, following up with the insurance companies and the state and federal agencies, matching up the coding from the ICD9 manuals—way too much paperwork for him. As he walked along the corridor leading to the locker room, he passed outside the attractive Asian patient's art studio. She was busy painting a portrait. It looked like a man with a long full mustache. She appeared to be working on his eyes.

As Greg continued walking down the hallway, he glanced up on the walls inside of the studio. They were covered with paintings. He couldn't help himself as he stopped outside of the long windows, purposely positioning himself so he stood behind her. He had been warned by another intern during an earlier training session not to bother Miss Kim. "She has special privilege and doesn't need people bugging her," he was told. From this position, Greg was certain that she couldn't see him. Greg crossed his arms and examined each painting hanging from the wall. There was one of a waterfall, a lake, a beach with crashing waves, one with planets, one of a horse, and still another one of a hovering hummingbird. Each painting was of professional quality and realistic, almost like a photograph. He noticed that, other than the painting she was working on, there was only one painting of people. *I wonder why?*

Hye-Jin was almost finished with her final painting. His face was complete. Only the eyes remained. She knew that painting the eyes was the most difficult aspect of a portrait, and she had purposely saved them for last. Many times, as in real life, the eyes are the gateway to a person's soul. As an artist, being able to paint the shape of the brow, match the eye orbit, the eye color, and the shine that reflects the light, a painter is challenged with these details when painting a portrait. If the eyes are not depicted exactly right, the entire portrait fails, regardless of how accurately the other aspects of the portrait are presented. In Hye-Jin's case, the image she had painted, his facial expression, had been one she had frozen in her memories. She didn't need a photograph to help her finish it. His face was a mental image she couldn't get out of her mind even if she had tried. For the last eighteen months during which she had been confined to this place, she had tried to clear her mind, but she couldn't. Those images were one of the memories that she associated with one of her greatest failures as a human—trusting the wrong person.

Having completed the basic formation of his eyes, she started to add lines on his forehead. She wanted to emphasize his expression of fear and surprise. She was trying to recreate the last image she imagined of her friend. In her mind, his death was all her fault.

But like many things in life, a person's mental recall of a situation may be flawed, such as the way eyewitnesses who are interviewed about what they saw at the scene of the crime. Many times, those statements given by witnesses are inaccurate. Around the world over, it is a well-known fact that law enforcement personnel prefer physical evidence over eyewitness testimony. Fingerprints, DNA, and fiber analysis are all reliable evidence, whereas eyewitness testimony is inconsistent, varying from person to person.

The recounting of an event is a mental image that the mind captures and stores inside the brain, a living organism that must strike a balance between abstract thoughts and reasoning, while simultaneously maintaining the physical wellbeing of the individual. People are tasked with maintaining a balance between the body and the psyche. As such, if an image or memory becomes too painful for the person to function, if cataloging and storing that image and memory begins to interfere with the person's ability to cope and function properly, the mind will defend itself by reformatting the memory, changing it and, in extreme cases even removing it from one's conscious thought.

During Hye-Jin's recent therapy session, her therapist had explained to her how brains work and why people lose their memories. He had tried to help her understand how sometimes dealing with memories prevents a person from being able to function normally. As she contemplated what he had told her, Hye-Jin stopped painting and relived one of those sessions.

*"You see Miss Kim, this is why it has been so difficult for you. Keep in mind, the brain is an amazing organ. It is tasked with the duty of orchestrating every function of the body. From digestion, breathing, blood circulation, and fighting viruses and infections, to the growth of new cells, hair, fingernails, toenails, and even one's eyelashes. The list goes on and on.*

*"Most of these systems are controlled at a subconscious level and do not require any purposeful thought. It is as if it is on autopilot. But in reality, there is no such thing as autopilot. It is the subconscious brain that orchestrates it all. It orders each particular cell of the body to behave and function. It controls the organism's temperature, heart rate, and breathing. The subconscious brain controls the pumping of the blood through the arteries and the creation of blood cells in the bone marrow. It*

*controls the electrical communication to each part of the body. Whether we understand how it functions or not, the brain is busy at work controlling everything, 24/7/365. It never stops. It can't. It doesn't have a choice. If the brain took a vacation, the organism would fail and die. Do you understand, Miss Kim?" asked the therapist.*

*Hye-Jin nodded her head.*

*The therapist continued. "We must also distinguish and recognize other functions that appear to be conscious and purposeful. Actions we perform with intent. They are not something that is done subconsciously. The best example is physical activity such as walking, throwing an object, singing, or speaking. Most people consider these behaviors as being within their own control. But that is only partially accurate.*

*"When the brain perceives an action or memory to be harmful to the organism, the brain may upon its own volition based on its own reasoning, choose to prevent a person from performing a physical action or block out a certain memory. Take physical injuries as an example. The brain may choose to mask out, temporarily preventing the conscious brain from making a voluntary physical movement and thus preventing certain muscles from functioning. This blocking is done to prevent the body from operating that area, giving the organism time to heal any damage to the injured area. This blockage of control is caused by the subconscious brain. It masks or inhibits certain muscles to a limb, for example, preventing the person from using it and causing further damage like when a person twists an ankle or breaks an arm.*

*"Similarly, the brain will mask, alter, and even delete memories that the mind has decided are too harmful and distracting to the subconscious brain. Keep in mind that the subconscious brain is tasked with maintaining a balance of all of its functions so that the organism may continue to function properly. However, sometimes, memories require too much energy and become too distracting to the subconscious brain. The brain understands its limitations. For obvious reasons, the subconscious brain never asks the conscious mind for permission.*

*Since infancy, the subconscious brain learned that the conscious mind is selfish, focusing on self-gratifying behaviors, behaviors that bring the conscious mind immediate gratification with only short-term highs. In many cases, those actions are detrimental and harmful to the organism. These imbalances can be seen in addicts, egotists, narcissists and thrill seekers. With these types of people, the immediate gratification is so important to the conscious mind that it will jeopardize the balance and wellbeing of the entire organism as it pursues short-term rewards.*

*"Most people are able to balance the needs of the conscious mind. Most people are able to find appropriate ways to experience excitement, gain personal recognition, and feel physical gratification through their interactions with the world, resulting in the natural production of chemicals inside of the body such as dopamine, adrenalin, and occasionally self-prescribed external things such as alcohol or drugs. Unfortunately, because humans perceive themselves as being in control of their physical worlds, they misunderstand the amount of control they really do have over their body. Although humans may be able to affect their physical appearance through exercise and body sculpting, they do not, for all intents and purposes, control the inner workings of their mind and the systems inside the body. Similar to the self-protective mechanisms the brain uses with physical injuries, it does similar things when dealing with memories.*

*"People do not consciously control their memories. Unlike recalling facts and figures from a mental database, images from real-life events are fluid internal pictures with complicated emotions attached to them. The mind understands how it encodes a real memory. But a real-life event that the conscious mind witnessed is altogether different. How the brain stores such memories has drastic consequences to the conscious mind. The subconscious mind, in this situation, is similar to a babysitter doing everything in its power to protect the child. The subconscious mind, like the babysitter, decides if it will allow the conscious mind, or in this analogy the child, to be exposed to an*

*event, like whether to allow the child to watch a horror movie, for example.*

*"The subconscious mind decides what it will allow the conscious mind to remember. To understand this concept is the key to understanding memories. Memories come from the subconscious mind. All memories are stored there. Any and all memories that the subconscious mind allows into the open, allowing the conscious mind to access, have been filtered and even edited to protect the organism.*

*"As such, when the subconscious mind chooses to suppress a memory, it has decided on its own, based on its unique understanding about the strengths and weaknesses of that particular person, whether that person is able to deal with the emotions associated with those memories. The subconscious mind must determine whether it will allow the person to dwell or relive the memory or whether this could be too disruptive to the subconscious. The subconscious mind must consider whether it will be able to work 24/7/365.*

*"This mystical mental gatekeeper has determined on its own accord whether it can afford to expend the necessary energy to suppress or alter the memory. If the subconscious mind alters or deletes certain memories, it will decide later if, when, and with what accuracy it will release those memories to the conscious mind. The conscious mind has no control here. The conscious mind is only allowed to influence 'certain' waking moments, but not all of them. The subconscious mind, unlike the conscious mind, is at work non-stop, all of the time.*

*"Your subconscious mind, Miss Kim, has been suppressing your memories about your past. Those events were so devastating and emotionally impactful that your brain chose to alter and temporarily delete them from your conscious memories. The psychiatric team has been working with you to help coax out those memories in an attempt to help you better understand why you have chosen to stay in the hospital all this time.*

*"Very similar to Eastern philosophies, the hospital has been utilizing hypnosis to try and tap into your subconscious. This*

*form of therapy allows a third party to interpret the reporting of those memories and help patients come to understand the situation from a different point of view. In your case, it has been working. You're showing signs that you appear to be feeling less burdened by your past, with less emotional attachment to those memories, which makes the pain seem less devastating. However, you have yet to fully and accurately retell us about those events. Your conscious mind is still in control, suppressing the memories," concluded the therapist.*

Hye-Jin took a deep breath. She picked up her paintbrush and began the last touches to the eyes. It wouldn't be long now. She was approaching that moment. She was about to finally remember what happened.

\*     \*     \*     \*     \*

Mike waited for the shuttle bus to pick him up at the arrival curbside area at *LAX*. His flight was uneventful. A non-stop flight from Lincoln, Nebraska, to *LAX*. The plane was close to capacity, packed with Mid-westerners heading to LA for their summer vacations. He was so engrossed with his own planning that he didn't notice the constant buzz of excitement as the passengers' conversations centered around their schedules and plans to visit *Disneyland*, see the *Dodgers* or *Angels* stadiums, *Universal Studios*, *Magic Mountain*, the beaches, Hollywood and the countless other attractions that drew so many tourists to Southern California.

Mike had already programmed Lee's—make that Cameron Sivesind's—address into his cellphone's GPS program. He had a reservation at the hotel. It was located the closest to Lee's house. Mike planned on driving by Lee's house before checking into the hotel. He would get a quick lunch and be on the lookout for a drive-through restaurant. Then he planned on driving by the church on Wilshire Boulevard near Koreatown. He would park across the street from Lee's house and wait. He still didn't know exactly what he was going to do, but his goal was to sit down first with Lee, and then with his fiancée and warn her. He had brought a photo album and newspaper articles about Lee's prior two wives. He needed to confront Lee about Annalisa's death and question him about the accidental death of his second wife. Also, why had he changed his name? Mike thought he knew the truth, but he had to give Lee a chance to explain himself.

The shuttle for the rental car approached the curb and stopped in front of Mike and many other passengers. Mike rolled his suitcase onto the bus and stowed it under the baggage storage area and then sat rigid in the seat nearest the door, contemplating what he wanted to accomplish over the next week. The bus doors closed, and a rush of air blasted out from under the bus as the driver released the air brakes. The bus began to accelerate toward the rental car areas.

If only Mike had a crystal ball, or had the power of clairvoyance, he would have just picked up his rental car and changed his plans. If only he could make the decision to "let it go." What good was any of this going to do, anyway? It wasn't going to bring Annalisa back. But Mike was stuck. His obsession over the loss of his sister had put him on a dangerous path. Lee had proven what he was capable of doing. Regardless of his recent change of heart—about which Mike knew nothing—there was no telling what Lee would do if confronted about his past. Mike knew Lee had plans. He'd changed his name, going so far as to prepare an escape strategy. Mike didn't know it, but Lee could grab his framed painting and cat sculpture and be on his way. But if Mike confronted him, there was no telling what Lee would do. It was never a good idea to corner a predator.

But life is about choices. The choices that Lee had made limited the roads he could travel, guaranteeing he would face certain challenges and obstacles. The old adage, "You've made your bed, now lie in it," had some truth to it. But up until now, Mike had only contemplated his suspicions about Lee. He had not taken that next step. He hadn't moved from a mental exercise into any real action. That all changed when he landed in LA. Now, with each step he took, Mike inched closer to changing his life forever.

But, that's life. People choose how to live their lives. The life of one person could be predictable and boring, while another might choose a life full of excitement and intrigue. Regardless of the path, each person will eventually face a decision, a fork in the road that could alter not just one life, but countless others. Like a drunken driver speeding down a main street, destined to cause a catastrophic accident, Mike advanced toward a point of no return. He still had a chance. He could still walk away. Or was it too late?

# 13

"I'm not sure, Jonathan. You know I'm afraid of water. I'm too scared. Let's do something else—on dry land." She smiled up at Jonathan, who returned her stare with a blank expression. He heard her words but could only focus on how impressive he would look with his hands on the steering wheel of the thirty-foot boat. He imagined the hull cutting through the smooth surface of the lake. He remembered her telling him the story of how she had almost drowned when she was only five years old.

She explained how her parents owned a small local fish market located just outside of Seoul City. She was so excited to be riding her father's motorized long canoe. The early morning calm mixed with the muted buzz from the outboard motor echoing off the calm *Han River*. The soft splash of the wake from the canoe washed up against the river bank. Hye-Jin loved these mornings. She treasured the beauty and peaceful moments alone with her father. His gentle manner and absolute unconditional love for her was evident. He cherished everything about her, and indeed his life revolved around her.

His entire being was focused on providing the best life he could for his little family, especially Hye-Jin.

As soon as she could talk, she had begged her father to allow her to remain sitting in the canoe until he had unloaded the fish. As the little canoe pulled up to the dock near their family fish market, she remained sitting on the front bench seat, gripping onto the narrow sides of the canoe. The river bank was shallow. The market was only twenty steps away. These early morning trips to the main fish market in Seoul required them to plan their trips so that they could return before sunrise. At that time of the day, the dock was deserted. Only the other business merchants and outdoor café workers stirred. As such, her father felt comfortable allowing her to enjoy the last few moments in the canoe before the market opened. As he lifted each crate of fish out of the canoe, he urged little Hye-Jin to be careful and remain seated. She smiled back and nodded her head. He stood and glanced back before carrying the fish crate toward the back door. She could hear her parents talking, and the unique sounds as the fish were pulled out of the crates, rinsed and then laid on a bed of ice to be displayed to the shoppers who would soon arrive.

She had been left in the canoe many times. Her father would only be away and out of her sight for a brief moment, less than a minute, as he walked inside the market, set the crate down and then returned to retrieve the other crates. On each return visit, he would smile down at his daughter and remind her to remain seated and hold on tight. But on this day, a large tourist ferry was passing by at just the wrong moment. The ferry's movement in the water created a bigger wake that sent large ripples across the river in both directions. As the weight of the last crate was lifted out of the canoe, the canoe became more buoyant and began an exaggerated bobbing, up and down, enhanced by the normal movement of the current.

As her father hauled the last crate toward the back door, he yelled back over his shoulder "Last one!" She knew it was almost time to get out of the canoe. As she waited for his return, she stood up and held her hands out, preparing for him to pick her up. She twisted her shoulders backwards and toward the direction he would be coming from. Her movements caused the canoe to tilt as her weight moved about. She lost her balance and leaned forward with a slight bend at her waist. The timing of her movements coincided with approaching rolling wave, which pushed against the side of the canoe and exaggerated the motion. As the wave continued to roll under the canoe, its force seemed to lift the canoe even higher, rotating the hull toward the shoreline as the wave passed underneath. It looked like a long narrow bucket being turned on its side to expel its contents. In one swift motion, Hye-Jin was thrown from the canoe into the frigid river.

She felt like she was being pushed over a cliff. With her outstretched arms, it was as if she were diving into the water headfirst. It happened so quickly that she was only able to expel a short muffled scream before entering the water. She had never swum before. Her thick jacket and clothing only worsened her situation. The bulkiness of her clothing acted like a sponge, soaking up the river water. She sank to the bottom within seconds.

As her father returned, he froze in his tracks. Where had she gone? He glanced back toward the market, and then back up along the deck. There was no one. He heard the blare of the ferry's horn break the silence and watched small waves splash against the shoreline. Glancing back at the canoe, he noticed it bobbing up and down from the passing of the ferry. He knew where she was.

Running toward the canoe, her father could see her bright pink jacket under the surface of the water. Immediately, he dove down into the shallow river's edge and pulled her up. Laying her on her stomach, he began to slap her back with an open hand. The force of his slaps against the wet jacket clacked out in a staccato noise that echoed in the silence. With tears rolling down his cheeks, he began pounding her back harder and harder. Hye-Jin's mother came out of the market to see what the commotion was. As she saw her husband pounding her daughter's back, and saw her waterlogged clothing, she

111

screamed in disbelief and ran to them and knelt at her daughter's side, grabbing her shoulders. Hye-Jin's small body began convulsing. With wide eyes, her parents held their breath as their daughter began coughing and spitting up water.

Her mother turned her over and cradled her small face in her shaking hands. With her face only inches away from her daughter's nose, she stared frozen, waiting for her to respond. Hye-Jin finally opened her eyes. They reached out and threw their arms around each other, clinging onto each other. Tears of joy and relief rolled down their faces. Screams welled up and subsided as they each began to calm down, but they never released their hold. As their breathing returned to normal, they began to notice the typical noise of the river. With the three still clutching each other, the noise from a car's engine broke their trance, the sound of gravel crunching against the asphalt as a car's tires rolled to a stop. Their girl would live. She would survive.

Struggling to stand, Hye-Jin's cold wet legs shook as she took her first steps. Squeezing her father's hand, she lifted her head. Her water-drenched hair fell in front of her eyes and hair stuck to her rose colored cheeks. The rocky river bottom had cut her inner lip, causing her teeth to take on a pinkish hue from the blood. Her grandfather had come upon the family huddled on the river bank, clutching each other tight. Hye-Jin could still recall his reaction: He ran toward them with his outstretched arms, grabbing everyone into a tight ball. Everyone knew who it was by the strong fragrance from the *Country Jasmines*. He began sobbing. As his body shook from his flooding emotions, he had held her tear-soaked cheeks between his hands and leaned down toward her face, his nose touching hers. She never forgot his words.

"You are special. You're going to make a difference in this world. I have so many experiences I want to share with you. This is not your time to go." Kissing her wet forehead, he stood up and breathed a sigh of relief. Bringing his arm up, he wiped his tears on his soaked jacket. He glanced back at Hye-Jin and whispered, "My princess, my special princess."

She explained that she would never go out on the canoe again. As she grew older, she never overcame the aversion of water in its natural setting. The closest she came to swimming was to sit in the public hot sauna Jacuzzi pools. She never learned to swim. The idea of having her head underwater made her hysterical.

\*   \*   \*   \*   \*

Jonathan had heard the story. As he looked into Hye-Jin's eyes, he knew she was reliving that moment. Just thinking about being near water did that to her. Jonathan closed his eyes, blinking back his initial response to try to convince her everything would be fine. He had plenty of time to do that later. He had already reserved the boat and had been bragging about it at work. He wasn't going to give her a choice. She could sit there in a life jacket, for all he cared. Besides, Yoshi, his Japanese counterpart, was always running his mouth off about sailing. Sailing was for sissies. Jonathan wanted the strength of an engine, like *NASCAR* on water. That was a manly sport.

Jonathan smiled at Hye-Jin and turned the conversation back to her restaurant, her menu, her workers—anything to get her mind off of the boat trip. Holding the glass door open, his mind returned to the boat. Jonathan smiled to himself. He was imagining how good he would look driving that big boat.

\*   \*   \*   \*   \*

Jonathan showed up an hour early. He had asked for an introductory training session on boating. He wanted to practice everything. He wanted to look as comfortable and confident as possible to impress Hye-Jin.

As Jonathan stepped out of his *Mercedes*, a young man in shorts and a white tank top approached him.

"You must be Jonathan Weed, right?"

"That would be me," smiled Jonathan. He glanced at the dock and the beautiful thirty-foot boat tied up, waiting for his morning session. His face beamed with excitement. An ear-to-ear smile appeared and remained the entire three hours. As they walked down the dock, the young man rattled off the specifications of the boat that Jonathan had already memorized. "She's got a 455 HP *Mercury* inboard/outboard with forged titanium prop. She's thirty feet, 6 inches, from stem to stern, and if we didn't have the governor on her, she'd hit 75 mph, easy like."

Jonathan and the instructor looked at each other, Jonathan with raised eyebrows and an expression of disbelief and admiration. "No shit?" He stepped over the rail, and his new deck shoes gripped the teakwood decking. As the instructor began climbing to the second-level captain's chair, he pointed to the flotation donut beside the ladder. Gripping his keys, the instructor unlocked the flotation device. Turning back over his shoulder, the instructor explained, "We have to lock these down. Some kids started stealing them. We have the oversized ones. They're two-hundred-fifty-pound capable." The instructor couldn't overlook Weed's size. "How tall are you, Jonathan?"

"Six five, three-hundred-fifteen pounds," he replied, looking down at his shoes somewhat self-consciously.

Continuing up the ladder, the instructor unlocked the upper deck floatation device. "It's cool. If you go in the drink, just make sure they throw you two donuts," he joked. Reaching the top, Jonathan glanced down and studied the donut. He made a mental note to make sure he unlocked the donuts. Hye-Jin was very fearful, of water and he wanted to make sure she was comfortable. "Are there any life preserver jackets?"

"Up here, right under the captain's chair. We've got some down below, under the back bench seat, as well." He held up the captain's chair to show Weed. Craning his neck, Jonathan could see the bright orange canvas life jackets and nodded in acknowledgement. He made a mental note to make sure Hye-Jin got one as soon as she came aboard.

The instructor sat in the chair and pushed the key into the ignition. Turning the key and pushing the start button, the engine came to life. The low rumble sounded like an ethanol alcohol dragster, waiting for the lights to drop at a quarter mile run. As they pulled out into the center of the lake and after all the basic safety issues were out of the way, the instructor had Jonathan sign the form confirming that he had been shown all of the safety requirements and that he had checked all the required boxes on the authorization form. Handing the clipboard back to the instructor, He gripped the steering wheel with one hand and held the throttle with his other. Pushing the throttle forward, he leaned into the wind rushing toward him and looked out over the bow. He would enjoy every minute that remained. He knew he looked awesome.

\* \* \* \* \*

"So what are we going to do today?"

"It's a surprise," smiled Jonathan. He decided to wait and tell her after they had arrived at the lake. "We're gonna have a great time." He had the picnic basket filled with only Korean cuisine. He had ordered the main dish from her own restaurant and stopped by the Korean bakery for some breads and fruit-topped cake. Everything was ready.

She knew that Jonathan was taking her on a picnic. He had asked her workers what she wanted. He had told them to keep it a secret, but her workers didn't take orders from a *"mi gook saram."* In fact, none of the workers liked him. They knew that if he hadn't been rich, their boss wouldn't even give him the time of day.

She wondered why he had on a polo shirt, shorts, and flip-flop sandals. He never wore those types of things. She had assumed that he must feel self-conscious about his size and avoided such clothing. Prior to coming to America, she had never seen such large people. It seemed that everything in America was bigger. The food proportions, the large superstores—even the grocery stores. She thought back to when she first saw the fruits and vegetables in America. They were enormous. Maybe that's why the people were so big, she pondered.

As Jonathan bent down to load her belongings into his trunk, she smiled as she examined his large back side. Afraid of offending him, she covered her mouth and turned her head so he couldn't see her face. Climbing into the car, she thought that he seemed a little too excited. What was he up to?

* * * * *

Mike had been literally stalking all known locations to find Lee.

Given the wedding, Cameron had been on the run with the rehearsal-dinner fittings for a tux and his traditional Korean attire. He also had his bachelor party that Barbara's husband had organized. It had been tame, attended by his teacher friends. No strippers, just drinks, expensive hors d'oeuvres, and champagne. All of the attendants had noticed a dramatic change in Cameron. Each had questioned why it had taken so long for them to get to know him. They really began considering him a close friend. For the first time, Cameron had felt the same. His life had somehow transformed. He was a new man. Meeting Hye-Jin had opened up his life to new possibilities.

The week preceding the wedding, Cameron had also been planning the honeymoon and began looking for a new home. With all of these random events, Cameron was on the go. Choosing not to stay with Hye-Jin until they were married, Cameron ended up staying several nights at the Beverly Hills Hotel. It reduced his time stuck in traffic traveling back and forth, going to all of these different events. Cameron was now set with his vacation request processed and approved, scheduled off for the next three weeks.

The randomness of Lee's schedule prevented Mike from having the face-to-face meeting that he had been longing for. His efforts had been thwarted. Mike's isolation and single-minded focus began to take its toll.

Mike had camped out in front of Lee's house for two solid days, dozing in the car and making drive-through fast food his staple diet and only refuge. He had developed a good rotation schedule for all of his meals, snacks, and bathroom breaks. As his surveillance of Lee's home continued, Mike found himself looking forward to those meal and bathroom breaks, if for no other reason than for the change of pace; McDonald's, Wendy's, KFC, and Jack in the Box. That was the order of his rotation for breakfast, lunch, dinner, and snacks.

By daybreak of the third day, Mike had had enough. He drove straight to a *Denny's* near his hotel, ordered a Grand Slam Breakfast with O.J. and decaf coffee, before scurrying back to his hotel for a normal nap in a comfortable bed. Mike's back and shoulders ached from being hunched down in the rental car, sitting for almost forty-eight hours straight. If he hadn't been able to watch Netflix from his unlimited *Verizon* smart phone, he would have gone stir crazy. He had re-watched the entire "Breaking Bad" and "Walking Dead" series. His arms swung low, and his eyes looked like small slits with bags under them as he made his way into his room. The effect of a full stomach accelerated his need for sleep. Kicking off his shoes and sliding out of his pants in a single motion, Mike dove onto the bed. He pulled down the blankets and slid under the covers. Only seconds after his cheeks touched the soft pillowcase, Mike dozed off into a deep sleep. His jetlag, coupled with the adrenaline rush from hunting down Lee, had finally taken its toll. Mike remained in a comatose-like slumber for the next ten hours. During that entire time, he remained in the same position, never rolling over to change body positions.

It was during that time that Cameron, a.k.a. Lee Fullem, had finally paid a visit to his own home. It represented the only chance Mike would have had to meet him face to face. The wedding was only two days away. He would have to catch him before the ceremony.

* * * * *

Mike awoke to a loud sound coming from outside of his room. A female voice was calling out and appeared to be banging her fist against the outside of his door. "Housekeeping!

Housekeeping!" He blinked back the urge to go back to sleep and started rubbing the sleep that had built up in the corners of his eyes. It wasn't until he heard the door open and someone coming into his room that he sat up.

"It's fine!" Mike replied. "I'm good. I don't need room service today."

"Oh, I'm sorry sir" the housekeeper replied. "We tried calling earlier, twice in fact, but no one answered. We even saved your room for last."

"I'm sorry, Miss. I was sound asleep and didn't hear the phone ring."

With that, the hotel housekeeper backed out of the room and closed the door. Mike looked at the digital clock on his nightstand. It was 3:00 p.m. This was his last chance. There was only one more day before the wedding. If he didn't find Lee today, Mike's only chance was going to be the morning before the wedding. With a new sense of purpose, he climbed out of bed and took a long, hot shower. All he could think about was food. The bathroom mirrors had accumulated a thick coat of moisture from his extended shower. Mike slid open the shower door and climbed out. Wrapping a towel around his waist, he walked into the room and sat on the bed. He reached over and grabbed his thick folder and began reviewing his notes.

For some reason, the news articles about his sister's death had lost their impact on his emotional state. He still missed her, but his anger and rage were gone. Unlike before, Mike no longer felt that uncomfortable obsession about what had happened. As he contemplated these new emotions, he came to realize that for the past ten years, he had been unable to do anything, unable to think about anything else except the notion that Lee had something to do with her death. But leaving his apartment, getting on an airplane, renting a car, and staying in a hotel—although it wasn't a traditional vacation filled with joy and excitement, it was a literal break from the monotony of his life. Even though he hadn't arrived at a resort destination or walked the beautiful beaches, the fact remained that he had given himself a mental break from his ordinary routine. He had allowed his mind to experience something new, meet different people, and do things that most people do as part of a vacation. Through that process, Mike found himself questioning why he was there. What good would it do, anyway? Nothing would bring back Annalisa. He was the only one in his family who hadn't moved on emotionally. Sadly, he found himself having to remind the rest of his family about her passing. It was as if she no longer mattered. Each time he did that, his family questioned him about picking an old scab and urged him to leave it alone.

Mike continued to ponder why he remained fixated, unable to let it go. He stood up, dressed, dried his hair, brushed his teeth, and walked out of his room toward his rental car. As he climbed into the car, he decided to go to the church. The wedding was tomorrow. He probably had a good chance of catching Lee there. He was right. Lee and Hye-Jin had just finished their last pre-marital counseling session and were taking a look at the church before meeting everyone in the wedding party at Hye-Jin's restaurant for a formal dinner.

# 14

"**H**oney," Hye-Jin said to Cameron as they walked through the church. "Remember, you'll be in this office until the priest comes to get you. Then, you'll walk with him and meet the best man and your groomsmen at the other end, under the cross," she continued, pointing out where Cameron should go.

"I know, I know. Just like we practiced yesterday during rehearsal, right?" Cameron said with a smile on his face and with a sweet teasing tone.

"Yes, just like that! Exactly like that," Hye-Jin joked back. "And I'm serious. I really don't want you to see me in the wedding dress until I walk down the aisle. I want everything perfect. I don't want to start off our marriage wrong. We don't need bad luck, right?" she pleaded.

"I understand, and I totally agree. I want to do this right. I want to do everything right from now on." Cameron replied. And he meant it. For the first time in his life, he was in love. He was the happiest he had ever been in his entire life. His relationship with Hye-Jin had started off slowly, but after the passing of her friend, everything had changed. She had been present when it had happened. Cameron had tried many times to explain to Hye-Jin that it wasn't her fault, that she couldn't have done anything to prevent it. It was just one of those things. Cameron was right.

Life is like a finite amount of energy. Each person is born with a clock that begins its countdown at birth. Some people are born with longer clocks then others. Some are given very short ones. Hye-Jin's friend had lived a good life. He was middle-aged and had a successful career. Cameron thought that the only regret her friend might have had was never marrying. At one point, Cameron had worried that Hye-Jin would choose her friend's affections for her above his own. He even had considered her friend a competitor for her heart.

In Cameron's prior life as Lee, he would have found her friend's passing a Godsend. But that was before. Cameron had changed. Hye-Jin's agony over his passing had worried Cameron. Her despair and sadness had affected him as well. He wanted to do anything to help her through those months. For the first time in his life, he was able to think of someone other than himself. He could feel her pain and felt compelled to help her through that ordeal. He checked on her daily, dropped by her restaurant throughout the day, accompanying her to the Korean movie theatre, subtitles and all. He didn't want anything from her; he just wanted to help. He wanted to take away her sorrow and guilt, the guilt that was so misplaced and unnecessary. He didn't care how much money she had and didn't expect anything in return. He just felt compelled to do his best to comfort her, to be a true friend, to see her back to her old self, to be happy. Cameron didn't understand why he had changed, but he knew he had, for the better.

As Cameron and Hye-Jin walked toward the altar of the church, she looked up to admire the large wooden cross mounted on the wall and recessed lighting that brightened the area. It was a perfect backdrop for their wedding. Hye-Jin looked up at Cameron, reached out her hands, and clasped his hands in her own. They stood motionless in the very spot where they would exchange their vows. She looked up into his eyes and smiled. "I'm so happy, Cam," she said in a soft whisper.

"Me too."

They were the only people still in the area. The priest had already returned to his back office, and everyone else had already left for the day. Under the beautiful towering arched ceiling, they hugged each other. They exchanged gentle peaceful smiles, the kind that only two people in love could exchange. These were looks that were known the world over.

This was a human experience; in exchanging their faith in each other, they were making a commitment to one other, sharing their dreams, and each striving to help the other become the best person possible. It was the selfless act of caring for another person more than oneself. Such absolute devotion toward another, that exchange of unconditional emotional attachment, creates a special bond. The mere act of a marriage ceremony isn't the indicator of true love. It is the unquestioning commitment toward each other's wellbeing and happiness that demonstrates the presence of true love. And that kind of love is unique. It is eternal.

In this case, the feelings shared between Cameron and Hye-Jin were real. They were soul mates who somehow, against all odds and beyond the boundaries of countries that were separated by the biggest body of water on the planet, had found each other. They had somehow been reunited through time, fortunate enough to stumble upon each other, being at the right place and under the right set of circumstances. It was real. It wasn't by accident.

Holding hands, they exited the church. With a soft gentle kiss on the lips, they said their good-byes. Hye-Jin was heading back to her restaurant, and Cameron had an appointment with his attorney. He wanted to update his will and add Hye-Jin to the deed to his house. As Cameron walked around the church toward his parked car, he noticed an old man sitting on the wooden bench next to the small pond, where a towering sprinkler was shooting multiple streams of water upward, after which the water returned to the pond in gently falling arches. The sound of the splashing water and the rush of the pressured spray of water jets was soothing. As he stood near some trees, he felt disappointed that someone was already sitting there.

The old man sat on the bench, facing away from Cameron, watching the water falling into the beautiful pond. As Cameron waited, deciding what to do, he realized he was ahead of schedule and didn't want to go to his attorney's office early just to wait in the lobby. He had hoped to get a moment alone before his appointment and spend some time here in front of the fountain. As he considered his options, he couldn't help but notice the condition of the man's clothes. They were worn and tattered. The skin on his neck was heavily wrinkled with a thick puffiness, as if he had spent many years weathering the outdoor elements. His hands were small, with short, stubby fingers. His wrists had deep lines and thick veins protruding through his sun-spotted skin.

The man must have noticed Cameron's shadow approaching from behind. Turning his head, he flinched backwards in surprise.

"Damn, man!" the man exclaimed. "You scared the shit outa me, dude!" he continued in a high-pitched, crackly smoker's voice. "You work here or something?"

"No, sorry. I didn't mean to startle you," replied Cameron. "I'm going to be married here tomorrow. My fiancée and I were just checking things out. You know, final preparations and all." For some strange reason, Cameron began to feel unsure, uncomfortable, unworthy. As he drifted deeper into thought, he walked toward the other end of the bench and sat down. Without realizing it, Cameron's demeanor had changed. Only moments before, he had been the happiest he had ever been. Then, without warning, he felt tired and anxious, on the verge of becoming sad. As he watched the ripples on the surface of the pond travel across the water, he seemed to forget about the old man.

"Wow. Dude, are you okay? What's the matter? Aren't you excited about getting married?"

"Oh, sorry, no. No, not at all." Cameron replied. "I've never been so happy in my life. I don't know what's come over me. Just a few minutes ago, I was all smiles."

"Maybe you're gettin' cold feet."

"No, that's not it!"

"Must be something? No foolin', buddy, you sure don't look happy to me." They both continued sitting on the wooden bench, taking in the moment. The street was empty. The birds were chirping as they flew between the nearby maple trees. The sky was cloudless, and a nice ocean breeze rustled the leaves in the trees. The weather was perfect.

Closing his eyes, Cameron inhaled deeply and let his shoulders slump forward as he exhaled. As he lifted his head, he glanced over at the old man, who was sitting upright and seeming not to have a care in the world. He appeared comfortable in his skin. There was no sense of shame or embarrassment. It was as if the old man's current place in life hadn't damaged his spirit. He exuded a sense of confidence and contentment. He was at peace. In contrast, there was Cameron, who would seem to have it all—savings, a good job, a good retirement, a house without a mortgage, and a beautiful, successful business woman whom he loved more than his own life and who was about to become his bride. So what was wrong?

As Cameron thought back on all the time he had spent with Hye-Jin and how happy she looked, it hit him. The flash of excitement and love that those memories brought were dashed away as he made the connection. Although emotionally this was his first time to feel the excitement of becoming a newlywed, he had seen it all before, twice before—except during those prior occasions, he hadn't felt anything. He had gone through all the motions, saying all the right things, doing all the things that newlyweds did. But neither time had he been emotionally connected. He hadn't been in love. It was all a show that he performed in pursuit of money. As this realization took hold, Cameron raised his hand to his mouth to cover the gasp that rushed out of his lungs. What had he done?

The full weight of his actions hit him with an undeniable force. The agony he felt was like a hot poker being thrust upward through his stomach and piercing his heart. Until that very moment, he hadn't realized how evil he had been. He remembered both his prior wives. They had genuinely loved him. They probably felt just like Hye-Jin did, just like he felt now. Before that moment, he had no clue. He had never understood their points of view. Until now, he hadn't understood the concept of love; the deep, overwhelming all-encompassing passion that one person could fell toward another. Also, he hadn't had the benefit of children. Otherwise, he would have experienced the deep care one feels while nurturing, teaching, protecting, worrying about, and devoting all of one's efforts toward the upbringing of another person. As that realization washed over Cameron, for the first time in his life he felt the gripping, agonizing, all-encompassing pain of regret and shame. His two past wives didn't deserve what happened to them. Their lives were cut short because of his insatiable greed and selfish mindset. Worse yet, they had been deceived by the one person in the world they believed had their best interest in mind; by the person who was supposed to love and protect them in sickness and in health. If they had married someone else, they would have had a chance to experience a long fruitful life. But Cameron had changed all that.

Without warning, great streams of tears gushed out of his eyes. Cameron began moaning a deep guttural sob that echoed across the once peaceful church courtyard. The birds retreated into the depth of the branches as the entire area became silent except for the sound of the water splashing back into the pond. Cameron's distress was so overpowering that only the clicking sound of his contracting esophagus could be heard as he continued to cry. His face was contorted, his mouth wide open, and his chest heaved up and down as he cried uncontrollably.

The old man watched Cameron. Although he didn't know the cause of his pain, he'd seen it many times. In some ways, people who have had the misfortune of living not just a long life, but one that involved homelessness as well, witnessing this behavior wasn't new. The old man had seen it when his friends had lost a loved one, lost a fortune, lost a job, lost something, something meaningful to them. He'd also seen it when they had done something wrong and felt deep remorse and regret for their actions.

Coming from the streets, part of the process of surviving there was to be reduced to one's lowest point, to have dreams shattered, and for happiness to be a concept that existed in their past and hopefully somewhere in their future. With a skill learned only through experience on the streets, the old man didn't shy away from what was happening. He'd seen the same thing played out countless times at the shelter, in the soup line, and in the alleyways throughout the downtown area of LA.

What he did next was almost an expected behavior, something the homeless did for each other all the time. It was called "doing a solid," being a rock for a fellow human, providing that person a friendly ear, or a word of advice, without passing any judgment; just being there, to comfort another human. So that's what he did.

The man slid across the bench, reached out his arm, grabbed Cameron's shoulder and pulled him close until the young man's face rested on his shoulder. Without control, Cameron pushed his face against the old man's arm and cried. Nothing was said. He just let it happen.

*     *     *     *     *

Mike pulled his rental car up in front of the church. It was located well off Wilshire Boulevard and ran adjacent to a large wooded park. The side street came to a dead end, so there was no traffic. He remained in his car as he pulled up in front and just stared at the church entrance. He didn't see any cars parked in the front. After waiting a few moments, he continued. Along the side of the church he saw two men sitting on a bench in front of a pond. The younger of the two seemed to be in distress and appeared to be crying on the older man's shoulder. Mike assumed it was probably someone mourning the loss of someone else, and he guessed that maybe there had been a funeral earlier. Mike slowed the car and tried to get a better look at them but felt awkward, as if he were intruding on their private moment.

The old man noticed a driver slow his car to a stop and stare at them on the bench. Although he was accustomed to attracting unwanted stares and pointing fingers by strangers who gawked in disgust at his presence, during moments like these, even the homeless deserved their privacy. The old man made eye contact with the driver and flashed the meanest expression of anger and disappointment he could muster, which clearly communicated to the driver that he was not welcome there. Through only the use of his body language, the old man urged the driver to move along.

After seeing the old man's reaction, Mike knew he wasn't welcome there and drove on, accelerating the car down the street. As Mike doubled back to Wilshire, he concluded that he would have to wait until the wedding day. As he pulled into KFC, he thought about what he was going to say to Lee once he found him.

*   *   *   *   *

Cameron had stopped crying. He kept his head resting against the old man's shoulder as he wiped his eyes and face. Once he felt more composed, he raised his head and spoke.

"I'm so sorry. I don't know what came over me," said Cameron as he slid his hand across the old man's shoulder wiping the fabric clear of his tears.

In a soothing, kind voice, the old man replied, "It's fine. We've all been there. We just have to pick ourselves up and put one foot in front of the other. One step at a time, one day at a time. No matter what it is, son, it'll get better."

"I wish it were that simple," replied Cameron. "I've made some seriously bad mistakes. I wish I could take them back, but I can't. What's done is done. And I can't do a damn thing to change any of it." Cameron remained staring at the ground with a look as if he were disgusted with himself.

The old man waited for Cameron to finish speaking. He hoped that he wasn't about to tell him all of the bad things he'd done in his life, and was grateful when he didn't. Only after he was sure that the young man was through speaking, did he interject.

"Well, let me say this. My two cents; take it or leave it." Cameron looked up, waiting for the old man to continue. "Life is special and beautiful. But it's challenging too. Sometimes a person can skate down the path of life with everything fallin' into place. While others, man, no matter what some people do, they get it wrong. And some guys, they get it way wrong.

I know I'm sitting in front of a church. But in my mind, regardless of what others say, I may not be the best Christian in this world, but by God, in my mind I am one. Even if I'm barely hanging on the end of the bus attached only by the tips of my fingernails, I am one. Now hear me out. This is where I lose some of my friends." The old man paused, looking Cameron dead in the eye for effect before continuing. "If all this forgiven stuff is true, which, shit, I believe, then why the hell are we only graded on our actions for this tiny sliver amount of time we have during our lives?

"I don't get it," said Cameron. "What do you mean?"

"What I mean is, if our spirits live forever, for eternity, why the hell are we graded on only the choices, decisions, and behaviors we did over eighty-plus years? If we're lucky enough to live that long, that is. That just don't seem right to me. I know, I know," the old man continued, changing his voice as if mimicking a child's whining voice, "It ain't in the bible." Returning to his normal speaking voice, the old man continued. "Some things aren't in the bible. Does the bible talk about *iPhones, NFL Football*, or *Q-tips*? Just 'cause it doesn't, don't mean they don't exist. Not everything is in the bible. Sometimes, we have to use common sense." Cameron smiled as the old man continued.

"So the way I figure, this infinity deal, you know, forever, you know the number eight flipped on its side, that symbol for infinity? Think about it. Forever is one hell of a long time, right?" The old man pursed his lips as he paused, thinking about his next thought before he continued speaking. "Take a piece of string. Tie that string to that tree right there. Can you see it?" With his hand stretched out pointing at the maple tree across from the pond, the old man paused, waiting for Cameron to reply.

"Yeah, I guess so."

"Well, now imagine that an inch of that string represents a lifetime on earth. Got it?"

"Yes."

"Okay. Now take the other end of the string. Now use your imagination here, and start running your ass off toward downtown. That's that like ten miles from here, right? Okay, now think about that same string going back even farther, let's say up to the—" The old man paused and his eyes rolled up in his head as he began thinking about something even farther away than that, before he continued speaking. "Yeah, the damn Moon! Now, shit, that's far, right?" He paused again for effect. In a louder voice, he continued "Wrong! Hell, that's nothin'. Infinity just keeps on going, my friend," he said with a smile.

"So let's take that same string and keep on going to the planet Pluto! Now, let's go past there too, to the next galaxy. Now that's far, right?" again pausing for effect. In even a louder voice, he said, "Hell no, that shit just keeps on going! Now picture that long piece of string. Now remember, each inch represents eighty years, got it?" The old man paused, this time with his eyes wide, looking Cameron waiting for a response.

"Yeah, I got it. I got it! One long fucking string," replied Cameron.

The old man smirked at his reply before continuing. "Yeah, long. So," the old man paused again to catch his breath and slowed his cadence in an attempt to make his point, "if life is so valuable, if life is so all important that our spirits live into infinity, the length of that long string, why the hell are we graded on only our actions for the length of one inch of that long-ass string?" With that, the old man stopped talking and looked into Cameron's face, waiting for a reply.

Cameron was taken back. He hadn't really thought about it too much. The old man had a point. The only thing he could say was "Huh?"

"Yeah, me too. Huh?" With that, the old man stood up and began walking away. "Crazy shit, right? Food for thought, though." he yelled over his shoulder. With one last turn, the old man faced Cameron and yelled, "Congratulations on your marriage, buddy!" then walked into the adjacent park and disappeared.

# 15

As Cameron sat in the attorney's front lobby waiting, he couldn't help but think about what the old man had said. He knew that throughout history, there had been much worse people than he, thousands of people who'd done much more terrible things. But the existence of those other people didn't soften the fact that he was a murderer. It didn't change the fact that he had been hiding from those deeds for over a decade, going so far as to legally change his name and to prepare an escape plan, should someone from his past come looking for him.

Cameron took a deep breath and a exhaled heavily as he contemplated his past. As he continued to wait to be called into his attorney's office, he was captivated by a reprint of famous Emanuel Leutze's painting, *Washington Crossing the Delaware.* Cameron's eyes were drawn to George Washington standing at the front of a wooden rowboat full of soldiers, crossing the ice-filled Delaware River with the American Flag waving in the wind. In his present state of mind and due to the recent conversation he'd had with the old man, he wanted to relieve his sense of guilt and shame. Cameron couldn't help but relate everything he saw as some reminder of his failures as a human. As he stared at the details of the wooden boat, it struck him that his treasure hiding in plain sight on the fireplace mantel was similar. His treasure was like a lifeboat, available for him to abandon ship and run again. The treasure gave him a means to start a new life somewhere else. It was his safety net and escape hatch. But by keeping an exit strategy, he would never be all in. Like when Captain Hernán Cortés landed in Veracruz back in 1519, Cameron had to do the same thing: He needed to burn his boat. He needed to get rid of the safety net he had created so he would be forced to succeed or die trying. The bad memories were also associated with his treasure. So getting rid of it was a way to walk away from that past life, and force him to build a new one. He needed to succeed or die. Keeping those ill-gotten items was eating away at his consciousness. Keeping them was a constant reminder of his past. Maybe, if he could get rid of them, he could free himself from the guilt that had begun to weigh on him, getting steadily worse. Only when he was with Hye-Jin did he feel at peace. Whenever they were physically apart, whenever he wasn't in her direct presence, interacting with her in some form or another, the guilt of his past would float into his consciousness. Like a troubled wayward spirit trapped at the scene of the crime, confined to the location where the spirit's final living moments took place, Cameron became haunted by the guilt of Lee's actions, and he would remain trapped for the remainder of his life.

The opening of the lobby door broke Cameron from his trance. An attractive young executive assistant stepped into the lobby. In Cameron's prior life, he would have noticed her expensive tailored suit, her designer heels, diamond necklace and engagement ring, as well as her Gucci watch. But now, he hadn't paid any attention at all. He didn't even notice. He couldn't have cared less.

"Excuse me, Mr. Sivesind? He'll see you know. Come this way, please," she said as she held the door open for Cameron. As he entered the long hallway, he grabbed his cell phone, turned down the volume, and then began scrolling through his contact list. Although he had changed and upgraded his phone countless times, he had been sure to transfer all the phone numbers and addresses to each consecutive phone. He wanted to know if someone from his past had located him and perhaps try to call him. Most honest people think differently. They aren't concerned about what to do if this happens or that happens. Honest people are very straightforward. They have nothing to hide.

But to lie successfully, that's a different story. Lying takes a lot of effort, a lot of planning. Like chess, a good liar must be able to think ahead, many moves ahead, to prevent being trapped. As such, Cameron wanted to know if someone from his past were calling. He would have to be able to answer the call as Lee, not Cameron. He didn't want to be surprised. He understood that most people are creatures of habit. He also understood that with the increased usage of cell phones as a person's principal form of communication, combined with the new trend of maintaining cell phone numbers throughout their life, even when moving from state to state, there was a high probability that most of the people would keep their same cell phone numbers. He was banking on this hypothesis.

As he followed the woman down the hallway, he continued his search in his cell phone directory and finally located the person he had been searching for. Arriving at their destination, the woman opened the door and announced Cameron's name to the attorney. This process made the customer feel important, but more importantly, it gave the attorney the proper heads up. Like any good law firm, they had a standard operating procedure when handling clients. They had hundreds of clients, but needed each one of them to feel special and important. Cameron knew the drill and expected the attorney to have a cheat sheet to keep him up to speed on each of his appointments.

"Hello, Cameron," said the attorney, flashing his whitened teeth. "How have you been these days? Oh, and, by the way, congratulations on getting married. That takes place—" he paused, looking down at a piece of paper in the folder with Cameron's name on it—"yes, wow, tomorrow!" Please have a seat. Do you care for a drink before we get started?"

"No, thank you; I'm fine. I have another appointment in about ninety minutes, and I know I'll hit rush hour, so I don't have much time." Cameron smiled. The attorney looked relieved at not having to engage in small talk. With a smile, he placed a blank yellow pad of legal-sized paper in front of him, held his Mont Blanc ballpoint pen in his hand, and prepared to take notes.

"The first thing I want to do is add my fiancée's name to the deed of the house, all of the checking accounts, and investment accounts," continued Cameron. The attorney stopped with a surprised expression on his face.

"You mean you don't want a prenuptial agreement?" he asked, incredulous.

Cameron thought about what his attorney asked. It made sense. Most marriages in California end in divorce. He had accumulated a sizeable portfolio and owned his home outright. The old Cameron would have demanded one. In fact, the discussion of a pre-nup would have been a requirement before even taking a single step toward marriage. But now, none of that mattered. He had changed.

"I know, right? But it isn't necessary. She is probably wealthier than I am. She's owned a profitable restaurant for years, has rental property, and was named the Business Women of the Year by the Korean Chamber of Commerce. If anything, she should be requiring me to sign a pre-nup."

"Are you sure, Mr. Sivesind? Getting one signed after the fact is not an easy matter. It tends to show your cards, so to speak, if we do," the attorney pressed. As Cameron nodded his head, the attorney contemplated the fact that the assets Mr. Sivesind had acquired before the marriage would be considered his separate property owned by the original owner and vice versa. He also knew that the passive appreciation in the bank accounts and real estate would not be considered active, thus indivisible in a divorce, either. But adding her name to his accounts and comingling these assets could get cumbersome in a divorce. He knew that having to calculate how much to allocate to each party would complicate matters—but, then again, it would mean more billable hours. With those quick mental gymnastics, the attorney was about to proceed when Cameron interrupted.

"Also, on another matter, I want you to arrange for some items to be delivered to a relative. And strangely enough, I feel that this second matter is more important than the name stuff. I need for you to have some items delivered to my relative, and I want them mailed out by the end of the day. I've been so busy with the marriage plans that it has gotten away from me. They will be in a crate that weighs about fifty pounds, so it's pretty heavy. It doesn't need to be insured separately, as I already have insurance on it." Cameron grabbed his cell phone number and read off the name, address, and phone number to the attorney, who scribbled the information down on his pad of paper.

"I know you're wondering why I'm asking you to handle this matter, and you must be asking yourself why I don't just drop it off at FedEx. Here's the issue. The address and phone number is the last known contact information I have for him. If you could please verify it and take care of that for me, it would be very much appreciated. And of course, I understand that there will be a charge for your time. This is an important matter and needs to be taken care of as soon as possible."

The attorney listened intently and didn't flinch. The name of his game was billable hours. He didn't care what he was being asked to do. If a client wanted him to be his expensive errand boy, so be it. At $200 per hour, this task would be better than dictating another letter and having to proofread it later for his signature. He actually was somewhat intrigued about doing something different. Without missing a beat, the attorney replied, "No problem at all, Cameron. I can have one of my guys pick up the crate later tonight. Does around six o'clock work?"

"Perfect!" Cameron replied. Just taking this small step of redemption seemed to lift his spirits. He was going all in.

"One last question, though, about the crate: No liquids or dangerous stuff, right? No guns or explosives?" the attorney asked, more serious than joking.

"No, not at all. It's a painting and a carving of a cat," replied Cameron.

"Okay, perfect. We'll take care of it right away. As for adding the names, we'll draw up the change authorizations and forms and we can have them available for your signature as early as next Monday," replied the attorney.

"That would be great. I really appreciate it!" With that, Cameron stood, shook his hand and helped himself out of the office. As he pushed the large double glass doors of the office building he considered whether he would include a note to Mike with the crate.

# 16

Hye-Jin looked up from her painting. It was complete. It was the exact image she held in her mind. It was just how she remembered him, with his sharp features and thick mustache. It even captured the surprised expression she imagined he would have had, just before he died. She took another thick brush and saturated it with black ink. In the bottom right-hand corner of the canvas, she wrote something in hangul, Korean script. She had never done this to any of the other paintings, just this one. She stepped back and looked at the image. She crouched forward so both of her legs were bent at the knees. Then, she sat on the floor with both her shins touching the cold tile floor. As she sat down while holding her upper body rigid at attention, with her bottom resting on top of her ankles and extended feet, she bent forward from her waist with her hands outstretched at full extension. She leaned forward until her face touched the ground and her outstretched arms and hands were flat in front of her. With her eyes closed, she bowed three times. As she stood, she opened her eyes, faced the painting, and spoke aloud.

"*Chaeso hamnida*," she whispered. Repeating her words, but this time in English, she said, "I'm sorry."

Taking a deep breath, she turned and began walking toward the counselor's office. She had another therapy session scheduled for 4:00 p.m. She was ready; today was the day. She was ready to return to her restaurant. She was ready to face her fears. She was ready to open up about what had happened. As she walked by the large window looking into the art studio, she glanced back at her paintings, but never stopped walking. There was no need. She had already spent too much time and energy hiding in that room, hiding from her past. She had made the decision weeks before. Today was the day. It was the anniversary of his death. It was also his birthday, well, their birthdays. They had both been born on the same day. It was time. She had already called ahead. Her restaurant manager was so glad to hear her voice. He had feared he would never see her again. She had asked him to pick her up at six o'clock. She was going to her final therapy session, eat her final dinner, and drink her final cup of tea before she left this place.

She turned down the hallway and approached the door. It was time to celebrate. Today was her birthday.

\*     \*     \*     \*     \*

Reggie had been standing in front of Jonathan's grave. He was thinking about how his life had changed since he had become friends with Jonathan. Although Reggie hadn't been orphaned, the circumstances surrounding how he had been raised made their upbringings similar. Reggie had learned to understand that the priest and nuns from Jonathan's life were similar to his neighbors, the Nuevos. Neither of them had been raised by blood relatives, but they had still been given the necessary love and guidance to become good people. Both Reggie and Jonathan had dominating physical appearances that gave most people the wrong first impression. At the same time, it was Reggie's appearance and the fact that he had killed a person with his own hands that protected him during the last nine years of his life. His first five years of incarceration were at the Youth Authority Facility. After turning twenty-one, he was transferred to an adult prison in Susanville, then released just before his twenty-fifth birthday. His prison counselors felt he had been given the short end of the stick and had done everything they could to protect him.

After his arrival in Susanville, and over the next four years, all those assigned to his case made sure that Reggie was only roomed up with physically smaller men with non-violent crimes. It worked. By the grace of God, he survived his ordeal unscathed. He had even completed his G.E.D. equivalency. The guards had been given their marching orders: "Keep an extra eye out for young Reggie." In their eyes, he was a hero. He had accidentally killed a pedophile junkie who was trying to molest his younger sister. During the assault, his addict mother lay passed out in her room, high on heroine.

Reggie had delayed sharing his story until after arriving in Susanville. He didn't want to mess up everything he had sacrificed for his family. Only after the Susanville counselor questioned him about why he hadn't shared this information with the police, did Reggie explain: He feared that if he told the truth, if the authorities knew about his mother, his brother and sister would be placed in foster care. He didn't want them to be separated, alone, and afraid. Reggie explained that even though his mother was an addict, his neighbors were like real grandparents. But because they weren't blood relatives and because of their advancing ages, they couldn't be certain they would be assigned permanent custody. And even if they were, there was a high probability of a significant delay. During that time, it was a certainty that both his brother and sister would be placed in the foster care system, where anything could happen.

Reggie didn't want anything bad to happen to any one of them. As such, he accepted the manslaughter charge. His court-appointed lawyer confirmed that because Reggie was a minor and with good behavior, he could avoid being sent to the adult facility until he was twenty-one. From there, he would be released no later than his twenty-fifth birthday. After meeting with the Nuevos, he set his plan in motion and lied, telling the authorities that he had gotten into an argument with his uncle and had used a wrestling move on poor Uncle Jim, accidentally breaking his neck during the struggle.

There was no mention of his mother's addiction nor her condition on the night of the incident. While still deciding what to do, the Nuevos had moved Mrs. Chambers into one of their back bedrooms and cleaned her room. The Nuevos and Reggie had talked it all out, understanding that this could go very badly for everyone if the truth were known. After discussing all of their options and thinking everything out, they rehearsed their stories before calling 911. During the sentencing hearing, Reggie stood firm and took the plea. He didn't want too many prying eyes looking into his home life. Accepting the blame, no additional investigation was done, which prevented any of the authorities from learning the truth.

After the Susanville prison counselor heard Reggie's story, and during the transfer process, Reggie was held in isolation, giving the counselor time to do some checking on his own. At first, he was skeptical. He had learned long ago that you never trust or believe a convict. To the counselor's surprise, though, Reggie had told the truth, every word. The beautiful thing about this terrible event was that his sacrifice had paid off. The apparent guilt over what had happened to him had changed Mrs. Chamber's life. With the support of the Nuevos and her boss, she did it. She came to realize how her selfish addiction had cost her son his freedom and had almost cost her daughter her innocence. That slap in the face was what it took. Although she still remained working and living in the same places, she was clean. After waking, and upon learning what had taken place, she made a promise to herself and to her children that she would change.

As Reggie wiped the headstone clear of debris, he placed a fresh bunch of flowers in the vase he had bought many months before. As he looked down at Jonathan's grave, he thought back to the night at the bar, the day Jonathan had become Reggie's best friend.

\*   \*   \*   \*   \*

"Excuse me, sir. Could I have a beer, please?" Reggie asked as he sat on one of the tall wooden bar stools.

"Sure, kid. What kind do you want?" replied the good-natured bartender.

"Up to you, Mister. It's my birthday, so make it a good one." Reggie smiled back.

The bartender walked toward the bar taps, reached into the refrigerator under the counter and pulled out a frosted mug. After positioning the mug under the tap, he grabbed the sticky beer tap and angled the mug beneath it as the golden liquid flowed into the container. With the skill of an experienced barkeep, he topped off the mug with the perfect amount of a foam head and slid it in front of the young man without spilling a drop.

"Let's see your ID first, Sonny," asked the bartender.

"Oh, yeah; right." Reggie handed the man his newly issued California ID. He hadn't been out of prison long enough to take the driving test, nor did he have a car, so the ID was fine. He had been taking the city bus everywhere.

"I'll be damned, you weren't kidding, were you?" asked the bartender, flashing his jagged coffee-stained smile.

"No, sir, I'm definitely old enough. I'm twenty-five years old, plenty old enough to drink legally, sir," Reggie replied, hoping the man believed him.

"No shit, son! That's not what I meant. I know you're old enough to drink. Damn, you're as big as an ox," he joked. "No, I mean that today's your birthday. You wouldn't believe how many cheapskates tell me that," chuckled the bartender.

"Why would they do that?" Reggie asked.

"You see, most bars give customers a free drink on their birthday."

"Really?" Reggie said, awestruck. "I had no idea bars did that! I was just making small talk, telling you about my birthday, sir. Seriously."

The bartender looked at Reggie up and down and started taking a closer look at this young man. He was clean cut and had no visible tattoos, so he deduced that the kid must be from some small town. As the bartender continued drying glasses with a tattered white dish towel, he looked back at Reggie and said, "It's okay, son." Smiling at the naïve kid, he said, "Happy birthday! That beer is on the house."

Lifting the cold frosted mug, Reggie smiled back. "Thank you, Mister."

It was the first time in his entire life he had been in a bar. It was the first alcoholic beverage he had ever tasted. As he sat at the bar enjoying his freedom, he saw a small table near the big-screen television with a large basket of peanuts. Seeing an opportunity, Reggie picked up his drink and moved to the empty table to watch the beginning of the baseball game. "I'm gonna sit at the table and watch the game, if that's okay, sir?" Reggie said.

"No problem, kid. Suit yourself, but enough with all the 'sir' stuff. That's what I call my dad. Just call me Benny."

"Yes sir—I mean yes, Benny!" Reggie smiled back as he made his way to the empty table.

As he sat down to watch the beginning of the game, Reggie felt a little self-conscious as he noticed a large mustached man on the upper area staring at him. The lighting was dark and difficult to see any details. He didn't want any trouble and tried to concentrate on the television, wanting to enjoy himself. Just as he started to make a good dent in the peanut bowl, he saw the mustached man who had been watching him rise up out of his chair and start walking toward his table. At first, Reggie tried to avoid making eye contact, but the man walked right up to the table and sat down. Tilting his eyes away from the television, Reggie finally made eye contact with the man.

"Hey, I know you," the man said with a big smile.

Waiting for his eyes to adjust to the lighting, Reggie's mind went into overdrive, trying to determine if this guy was a threat. Spending the last nine years of his life incarcerated, Reggie had developed a second sense and the keen ability to assess a person quickly. As he looked up and stared the man, it hit him. It was Jonathan from the church.

"Oh, hey, Mr. Weed. Funny seeing you here," Reggie smiled.

"Hey Reggie, did I hear you right? Is today your birthday? Really?" asked Jonathan.

"Yes sir, Mr. Weed," replied Reggie with a big grin, relieved that it was a friend and not an ex-con from prison who had recognized him.

"I'll be damned. Small world, huh?" Looking up at Reggie, Jonathan pulled out his wallet, slid his license out, and tossed it across the small table. "Mine too!" Jonathan smiled.

Reggie picked up the license. It was true. They had the same birthday. "No shit," muttered Reggie as he cracked a huge ear-to-ear grin. "Well Mr. Weed, happy birthday! I'd be honored to buy you a drink, sir."

"Oh no, young man, not in this lifetime. The drinks are on me!" replied Jonathan.

"Are you sure, Mr. Weed?" asked Reggie.

"Come on Reggie, who we kidding? I'm the guy who drives a *Mercedes*, right?" he joked.

Reggie thought, *he's right.* With a twinkle of envy and excitement, Reggie said, "Boy, that's a beautiful car, Mr. Weed."

"Enough with 'Mr. Weed.' Call me Jonathan. I'm gonna order us some steak sandwiches. You hungry?"

"Yes, sir," smiled Reggie.

As Jonathan walked to the bar, Reggie felt blessed. This was turning out to be his best birthday ever. As he turned back to watch the first inning on the big-screen television, he gulped down another drink of beer and was fascinated how well it complemented the taste of the peanuts.

\* \* \* \* \*

Reggie sat in his black *Mercedes*. Although it stood out among the other vehicles parked at the modest apartment complex of only one- and two-bedroom units, it never bothered him. But this morning, as he sat in his assigned covered parking space, he began to feel the burden of the gift, the burden of what his best friend had asked him to do. He'd read through the large envelope that was left in the glove box. Reggie's grip on the leather-covered steering wheel tightened as he contemplated his situation. He hadn't taken the evidence contained in the envelope at face value. He spent some money and had a private investigator check it out. The PI confirmed that it was all true.

Reggie never discussed the matter with anyone. This time, no one else could be involved. He wouldn't risk the possibility of someone finding out what he planned. He refused the chance of implicating anyone else in case he was caught. Reggie considered the fact that he had spent most of his adult life incarcerated for a crime he had in fact committed. However, had all of the circumstances been known, he would have been exonerated. But if that had happened, the lives of his mother and siblings would have changed forever. This time, what he had been asked to do was altogether different. This time, it wasn't an act of protecting his sister. There was no easy way of putting it. To go through with this, was an act of cold blooded murder.

Reggie looked down at the *Mercedes* emblem on the steering wheel and began thinking back to that night at the bar; the night he and Jonathan had become best friends. The night he learned about Cameron's past.

*     *     *     *     *

"I'm telling you buddy," Jonathan said in a slurred voice. He had already drunk five beers before he had joined Reggie's table, followed by four celebratory shots of *Jack Daniels* since arriving at the bar an hour earlier. Reggie had declined both of Jonathan's offers for a special birthday toast, electing to stick with beer. Reggie had refrained from overdoing it. It was his first time drinking alcohol, and he was still on parole. Technically, he was only advised against becoming intoxicated in public. Although his counselor had discouraged him from visiting these types of places, by the letter of the law, he had not violated the conditions of his parole.

Jonathan's face was now tilted downward in an exaggerated slump of his shoulders. Despite his large size and the steak sandwich he had eaten earlier, he had consumed more alcohol than his body could process. It was a simple matter of biology and physics. A typical two-hundred-pound male's body could process one twelve-ounce beer or a four-ounce shot of alcohol an hour. Because Jonathan was over three hundred pounds, he could process fifty percent more. It was true that some people could control their motor skills, speech, and facial features better than others. This apparent tolerance contributed to the notion that some people could handle their alcohol consumption better than others. Regardless of how an individual perceives their tolerance or not, it was a scientific fact that alcohol impairs a person's ability to function. In Jonathan's case, he was well down the road to intoxication as he finished off his sixth beer and waited for this next one to arrive. The bartender had already put Jonathan on his watch list but knew him well and appreciated his excessive tips. He would extend Jonathan a longer leash than he allowed most other patrons.

"I'm telling you Reg," Jonathan continued. "Life's a bitch, man. Go figure. Why would she choose that dweeb over me, huh?" Looking at Jonathan's condition, Reggie couldn't help but display a slight smirk and smile. It wasn't difficult for Jonathan, even in his inebriated state, to catch the meaning behind that smirk, and he spoke before Reggie could respond.

"No, serious, good buddy. I'm not normally like this. Today's my birthday right? And I'm trying my best to deal with the fact that the girl I'm head over heels over is leaning more toward this school-teacher guy. I'm not saying it's over or nothing. No, no, no. Nothing like that. In fact, I've got a huge date tomorrow night with her. It's all planned out. I've rented this awesome boat, huge thing. I'm gonna take her to Pyramid Lake, technically a reservoir. It supposed to be the best lake in LA, about an hour north on I-5 near the Grapevine. We're gonna watch the sunset and everything. It's gonna be awesome." With that, Jonathan stopped speaking and turned away from Reggie, as if he was struggling with sharing something.

Reggie took the chance to interject, "Mr. Weed, you're a great guy. I'm sure you aren't like this all the time. I understand that today's a special day and all."

Jonathan turned back toward Reggie and leaned in close, placing both his elbows and forearms on the table, and looked into Reggie's eyes as he continued speaking, but in a whispered voice.

"You see Reg," Jonathan continued. "I'm not proud of it, but in my business, you don't trust the other guy. You see, love is like business. It's survival of the fittest. It's a dog-eat-dog world. So you know, you got to know your competition, right?" He looked at Reggie more intensely and leaned in closer. In a whisper, he said, "And man, this dude came up bad apples, man, *no bueno.*"

Reggie stared back blankly, waiting for Jonathan to continue. The silence dragged on as Jonathan contemplated speaking any further. Intrigued, Reggie couldn't help himself and urged him to continue.

"What did you find out?" Reggie asked.

Jonathan turned his head to make sure no one was approaching. Then, he looked over Reggie's shoulder to make sure no one was close enough to hear what he was about to say. After satisfying himself on that count, he continued.

"Before I say anything Reg, you got to swear to me, man, on your death bed, okay? I'm serious. As God is your witness, not a word to anyone," Jonathan said.

"I swear, Mr. Weed," Reggie replied. "As God is my witness, I won't say a word to anyone. Not in a thousand years," he replied, while holding up his right hand.

Jonathan sat up tall in his chair. His facial express had changed as if, at that very moment, all of the alcohol that he had consumed had somehow vanished from his system. In a calm and sober manner, he leaned in so close to Reggie's face that Reggie could smell the alcohol when Jonathan exhaled. In a soft whisper, Jonathan spoke. "He's a murderer."

Hearing those words, Reggie felt a sense of guilt and shame. Tilting his head down, he thought about what Mr. Weed would think of him if he knew what he'd done. Lifting his eyes back up at Jonathan, he continued to listen. He didn't know what else to do.

Seeing the effect his words had on Reggie, Jonathan knew he had to clarify what he meant. He already knew Reggie's story. As a senior church volunteer, he not only knew his crime but had met his parole agent. Jonathan had all the juicy details about Reggie's case. Like others, Jonathan agreed that Reggie was a hero.

"No, Reggie. Dude, I'm not talking about you. I know your case," Jonathan said. "You're different. You were protecting your sister. You took the fall for your mom. Dude, you're a hero man. Seriously, my young friend, this is no reflection on you, buddy. Okay?"

Reggie was surprised that Mr. Weed knew. With a sense of relief, Reggie looked up at Jonathan and replied, "Thanks, Mr. Weed. I really appreciate it. What did this guy do?"

Jonathan explained. "This bastard killed his first wife. Then, moved from the Mid-west and changed his name. Then, he leaves his next wife to die in a fire. Although both of these deaths were deemed accidents, I know better. The numbers don't add up. Once? Maybe. Twice? Very unlikely. Then you throw in the facts that he changes his name and never had children, I call 'Bullshit!'" now raising his voice slightly. Realizing what he'd done, Jonathan regained his composure, leaned forward, and continued in a whispered voice. "I'm telling you Reg, you'd have better odds winning the lottery than all that happening by chance." With that, Jonathan leaned back in his chair, grabbed the beer that the hostess had just delivered to their table, tilted the mug to his lips, and took a long draught.

\* \* \* \* \*

The noise of the car door slamming shut next to him broke Reggie from his trance. He glanced back toward the envelope sitting on the passenger's seat. He had been procrastinating for months. When the PI told him that Cameron had become engaged to the same woman Jonathan had loved and that the wedding date had been set, he had been racking his brain trying to decide what to do. Nothing came. Each day, he had hoped for some divine intervention. But there was nothing. Now the wedding day had arrived.

Reggie pushed the keyless ignition button. The gentle rumble of the engine came to life. He backed out of his space. As he drove out of his apartment complex, he went into auto pilot. He'd been driving to the church every other day for the last several months. He knew the route by heart. As he turned on the radio, his mind drifted back to the last words he'd had with Jonathan.

# 17

Hye-Jin sat in a comfortable leather chair. She preferred it to the lounge chair that was available as another option. Like her prior sessions, she was asked to close her eyes and to take deep breaths. Any moment, the therapist would begin to count out loud backwards from ten. As she counted, she would coax Hye-Jin into a deep state of relaxation. The therapist began to speak, "Ten."

With her eyes closed, Hye-Jin concentrated on the therapist's voice. "Continue to take deep breaths. With each number I call out, imagine descending underground. With each descent, you will feel more relaxed than before. Now, imagine entering an elevator. Turn around and push the button with the arrow pointing downward. I want you to envision the elevator doors closing and the compartment descending downward fifty feet," said the therapist in a soft, soothing whispering voice.

"Nine," she continued. "Now, imagine dropping downward twice as far. You're now one hundred feet below the surface. It's darker and quieter than before. Take another deep breath," the therapist urged. "Now, slowly, exhale. You're becoming more relaxed. Your arms are getting heavier," she continued taking the volume of her whispering voice down ever so slightly. Hye-Jin could hear the therapist's voice. It was still strong and clear.

"Eight," continued the therapist. "I want you to imagine descending ten times as far in the elevator. The compartment is even quieter and darker than before. I want you to take another deep breath. Your arms are becoming heavier than before. You're becoming more relaxed."

The therapist continued coaxing Hye-Jin downward. It had taken over a year of weekly sessions before she had stopped resisting the process. With each session, she became more accustomed to the ritual. One day, her conscious thoughts, which had before now been interfering through constant judgmental interpretations and evaluations, stopped. As she began to remember past events without those critical self-examinations, her subconscious mind seemed to be allowing the suppressed memories to surface in their true unfiltered format.

After reaching the last level, the therapist prepared Hye-Jin to go deeper than they'd ever gone before. Her goal was to set the stage so that her mind wouldn't fear opening up and examining those memories. After countless sessions, the therapist urged Hye-Jin to break through. Everyone on the medical team was in agreement: She was ready. It was time. And more importantly, it appeared the Hye-Jin wanted to tell her story, to explain what had happened and what she had experienced.

"Now," whispered the therapist. "It's time. Let the doors open. We've been to this spot many times before. It's the white room you described. You can see the table in the center of the room. On the table, there is a strong, thick metal can with a lid on top. You can see the details of the lid. There is a big handle, so big that you could grab it with two hands. I want you to imagine walking closer to the table and can. Now, place both of your hands on top of the can and grab the big handle with both hands. Now, look at your hands. Can you see them, Hye-Jin?" asked the therapist.

"Yes," she replied.

"Good. This time, it's different. Today, the lid is not screwed down. This time, the top is sitting unsecured on top of the can. The pressure inside of it appears to be pushing the lid off. It will take very little effort to open it. Can you see it? Can you feel it?"

"Yes," replied Hye-Jin. Then the therapist paused. The room went silent. Hye-Jin and the therapist seemed to be holding their breath. The silence was deafening. Waiting seemed to intensify Hye-Jin's anticipation. The delay and extreme silence was intended to magnify the experience. Hye-Jin continued to wait to hear the therapist speak. Why wasn't she giving Hye-Jin her next instructions? The anticipation began to boil over. Her natural instinct was to respond to the therapist's instructions. But there were none. By design, the delay had been extended. They needed a way to take advantage of a persons' need to react; the uncontrollable urge to respond to the next obvious instruction. Hye-Jin had reached that place where she was no longer consumed by guilt and regret. She was no longer weighed down by feelings that prevented her from moving forward. It was time. With that, the therapist gave her one final push when she said, "When you're ready, raise the lid and tell me what's inside the can."

Without further coaxing, both of Hye-Jin's arms raised above her head. Without any hesitation, she began to speak. This is what she remembered.

\* \* \* \* \*

"Jonathan drove me to a lake about an hour outside of Los Angeles." She spoke in a choppy, robotic fashion, as if she were relaying the facts only. No emotion seemed to be associated

151

with her words. "When we arrived at the entrance, he drove down to the dock area. He parked the car and we got out. I helped him carry things down. I carried the basket of food toward the lake." She paused and seemed to gather her thoughts.

The therapist, as she had done before, was recording the session. These recordings not only helped address the patients' situations, but also allowed the entire staff the opportunity to view each other and provide additional insights and feedback. The therapist glanced up at both cameras and could see the steady green light glowing downward. She was confident that everything was working properly. She wanted to make sure that everything was recorded.

"There were many people waiting near what I thought was a dock. They must have been part of a catering company, because there was more food, drinks, and desserts displayed." The therapist noticed a slight increase in the pace in which she spoke. The patient's facial expressions became more exaggerated and animated as well. "I was offered a seat at a table and another person brought me a tall glass of wine. It was a chardonnay, my favorite," continued Hye-Jin. Her words quickened and she started using her hands as she spoke. The volume of her voice increased again. Not reaching the level of a shout, but a definite rise in her speaking volume. She continued.

"It happened so quickly. I wasn't expecting it to happen. One man approached me with a vest of some sort. It was bright orange. I first thought it was a gift from Jonathan or something. While Jonathan held my wine glass, the man slipped it on me. I was so preoccupied with the wine glass and the orange garment that it didn't occur to me that I was being directed toward the platform on the water. At least I thought it was a platform."

Hye-Jin paused, held one hand to her lips and turned her head away from the therapist as if she were contemplating that memory. After a short pause, as if she were confident in its accuracy, she continued to speak.

"Another woman, she was waiting by the entrance to the platform. She had held what appeared to be a small gate. She stood there holding it open so I could walk through it. She reached out, held my hand so I wouldn't lose my balance. I stepped out onto the platform. There were several men on the platform talking to Jonathan as we walked onto it. The platform was very comfortable looking. It had plush cushion chairs positioned around the outside edge of the entire platform. It looked very expensive and luxurious.

Hye-Jin paused, tilted her head down and stretched both of her arms out. Her hands were facing downward as if she were patting the air as she described the cushions. After a brief pause, she continued in a soft, gentle, relaxed voice.

"It was a beautiful moment: The water, the comfortable platform, the food, drinks, and attendants; everyone smiling, especially Jonathan." She paused. Placing both of her hands back in her lap, she looked up at the therapist and smiled. After a brief pause, she said, "I didn't even realize we had pulled away from the dock. Jonathan must have been standing in front of the steering wheel. I hadn't noticed it at first. It wasn't like a car. You didn't have a brake or accelerator pedal on the floor that you needed to operate. You could drive it while standing. Jonathan just pushed a lever down and directed the steering wheel.

"He kept smiling at me. I could feel the wind on my face, but he kept the speed slow, no abrupt turns or sudden movements. It was like gliding on a lake of glass. The boat remained calm. I couldn't feel any rocking. It felt wonderful. I felt safe and relaxed." Hye-Jin closed her eyes and extended her arms out to her sides. With her eyes still closed, she continued speaking.

"I turned my head toward Jonathan, and he continued to watch me. I could sense his concern for my feelings. He knew about the accident I had as a child. I could tell that he was worried that I would be angry with him for tricking me," she said, in a cute, joking manner.

153

"But I wasn't mad. I wasn't even afraid anymore. I felt exhilarated. The memories of those wonderful times with my father on our canoe; those feelings came flooding back into my mind. Jonathan told me then that he had rented the entire lake until sunset. It was just the two of us on the lake; no one else. It was so peaceful. It felt amazing. He continued driving the boat to the far side of the lake and began turning it around. The boat was very long. I was told later that Jonathan had misjudged the distance that he needed to complete the turn. He had to reverse it and angle it back and forth. I could see his surprised face. I could tell he didn't want to scare me. He was more concerned about my feelings. I think that's how it happened." Hye-Jin's head dropped down. Her shoulders turned inward and her back curled forward. She took a deep breath and looked up at the therapist before she continued.

"Jonathan finally got the boat turned around, and we were gliding back in the opposite direction. He must have been more concerned about me…. He should have been looking forward…. If he had, nothing would have happened."

Hye-Jin raised her hand to her chin. A single teardrop pooled in the corner of her eye, then tumbled down across her cheek. The therapist watched without interrupting. "To make the turn, he had gotten too close to the shoreline. If he had been looking forward, not at me, he could have ducked. At first, I didn't know what had happened. I just heard a loud roar from the engine as the thrust of the motor kicked into full throttle. The boat lurched forward and accelerated. I grabbed the side of the boat with both hands. I must have closed my eyes."

She sat in the leather chair, gripping the armrests as she continued. "I screamed. The wind began to rush into my face, blowing my hair backward. The boat went faster and faster. It happened so quickly. I was scared to move. I looked over at the steering wheel and—" Hye-Jin paused, her voice softened. In a whisper, she said, "He was gone." She sat in her chair, with both her arms wrapped around herself, as if she were trying to warm herself. Her voice drifted off, the volume dropping off to be almost completely inaudible. Only later, after the therapist watched the taped session, where the technicians were able to increase the volume when the recording was replayed, could she hear what Hye-Jin had said. She had repeated, "He was gone."

The therapist sat motionless. She didn't want to say a word. She didn't want to interrupt. She had seen it countless times. Once the floodgates of a person's mind opened, it would all come out: every last word; everything. She stared at Hye-Jin to see what she would say next.

After contemplating her words, Hye-Jin was confident that she had explained it accurately. It was typical in these situations. Many times, when a patient retold their story, they were actually revisiting those once hidden images. The patient wouldn't appear to be upset. Likewise, many homicide detectives report that the accused would recount their grisly deeds as if they were reading a grocery list. Their voice would reveal no emotion whatsoever. The therapist and Hye-Jin's medical team, with all of their combined years of knowledge and experience, had concluded that the subconscious brain would disengage from the conscious brain during times of a confession. Otherwise, the conscious brain would try to rationalize, justify, and attempt to place blame during the retelling of the events. This temporary separation of control probably accounts for so many criminals' recanting their confessions after they later realize what they've said. But this was no criminal investigation. The therapist patiently waited for Hye-Jin to continue speaking.

"I remember speeding across the lake. The engine noise became louder and louder, reaching a mechanical screech with a throaty sound that boomed out across the lake and bounced off the nearby mountain range. The lever had apparently been pushed downward full throttle, so I was told later. I glanced up, my mind trying to reason through some way out of the situation. I was frantic, looking for anything. Then, I saw it. I didn't know if it would work, but hoped it would. In my fear, I saw a key on the boat consol. I was hoping that boats worked just like cars. In that split second, I urged myself to find the courage to stand up, walk forward, and grab and turn off the key."

Hye-Jin glanced up, away from the ground, and looked into the therapist's eyes before continuing. "It worked. When I turned the key, the engine stopped. It took several minutes for the momentum of the boat to slow down. The boat finally did slow down, eventually coming to rest floating on the lake. I just sat there on the boat, alone. I don't know how long I sat there. I was frozen in fear." With a shrug of her shoulders and with a deep exhale, she continued. "I just don't know how long I sat there."

After a brief pause she spoke. "I can't remember how I got off the boat. But I do remember sitting in one of the chairs that had been placed on the dock before we left. Someone wrapped a blanket around my shoulders. I was still wearing the orange vest. I could hear one of the men talking to a police officer. He explained that Jonathan must have hit a low-hanging tree branch near the shore. Jonathan was very tall, six feet five inches tall, so maybe that had something to do with it. A branch must have knocked him overboard. They found a spot of blood near the front window of the boat. They believe that he must have hit his head and been knocked out. They said that most likely, the throttle must have depressed as he fell overboard, which caused the boat to accelerate. The man explained that they heard the boat go full throttle. At first, they thought he was showing off, but he hadn't been." She paused somewhat winded from speaking non-stop for several minutes. After gaining her composure, she continued speaking.

"They found his body just after sun fall. He had drowned."

\*   \*   \*   \*   \*

The therapist covered her own mouth with her hand, pinching her nose with her thumb and index finger. The discomfort and literal covering of her mouth was her way of preventing her from interrupting. She didn't want to make that mistake. She had seen it so many times. Having had the opportunity to review other sessions with other therapists so they could each critique the efforts of their colleagues, the biggest faux pas was when the therapist interrupted the patient. It had become the cliché of mistakes. Each time they saw one of their colleagues do it, a communal groan could be heard. She was using all of her willpower to remain quiet, to avoid the impulse to interject a thought, to ask a question. Her twelve years of experience were paying off. Later, her colleagues would commend her for remaining objective and unfazed. To her own surprise, she sat still to see what Hye-Jin would do next. After several minutes of awkward silence, she watched Hye-Jin fidget in her chair, until she finally continued speaking.

"It was devastating. To go from elation and feeling proud for overcoming my fear of water to being a passenger on a runaway boat, then to be present when one of your best friends dies." After a brief pause, she continued. "If it wasn't for Cameron, I don't know what I would do."

"Who is Cameron?" asked the therapist, almost biting her lip the second she had uttered the question. Closing her eyes, the therapist chastised herself for interrupting Hye-Jin and possibly stalling her train of thought. Clenching her fists, she hoped that she hadn't ruined everything. Holding her breath, she waited to see what happened.

Unfazed, Hye-Jin replied, "He was a friend of mine, at the time. When he found out what I'd gone through with Jonathan, he wouldn't let me out of his sight. He would call me, drop by my restaurant, he would stay late and just talk. I guess it was natural, spending that much time with each other. We became inseparable. We went to movies, mostly the Korean subtitled ones. He never complained. He became my best friend." After a brief pause, Hye-Jin looked up at the therapist and said, "We fell in love."

The therapist was shocked. Over the course of the last eighteen months of treatments, no one had any of this information. Up until today, they were only aware of a childhood boating accident, as well as minute fragments of her past. That was it. But today, she learned about her two friends,

Jonathan and Cameron. One who died and the other one with whom she'd been in love. They also learned that she owned a restaurant. The therapist's self-control was being challenged more than at any time in her professional career. She focused on remaining an objective listener; she would not make the same mistake twice. Waiting to hear more, the therapist was immediately rewarded for her efforts as Hye-Jin continued.

"But it was all an act. He had lied. He only wanted my money. In fact, he'd done it before. He'd even gone by a different name too. I saw the pictures of his two other wives. They were pretty. I wish I had never met him."

Hye-Jin stopped speaking. She sat tall in her chair and crossed her legs. Her body language said it all. She was finished chastising herself for what had happened in her past. What was done was done. With a nod of her head, she crossed her arms and announced to the therapist, "We're done here. It's time to go home." She didn't even wait to be eased back from her trance. Breaking out of her trance, she stood and walked to the door. Before the therapist knew what hit her, Hye-Jin had walked through the door and watched the door close behind her. In the isolation of the room, sitting by herself, the therapist finally spoke. Her peers would all laugh upon hearing her words during its replay as she said, "Holy Shit!"

# 18

Mike was sitting in his rental car drinking his second Big Gulp drink. He had parked down the street, around the corner from the church. He could see people coming and going through the side entrance. He chose not to park in the lot adjacent to the church to avoid being boxed in. If his suspicions were accurate, confronting Lee could escalate to chaos. As Mike continued his wait, he could see water from the fountain spraying high up into the air before cascading down into a large manmade pond below. Just the day before, he had seen two mourners comforting each other as they sat on the bench in front of the fountain. From prior visits to the church and through his past research over the Internet, he knew today was the day. To help him pass the time, he turned on the radio and found *KLOS*, a local rock station. He kept his windows rolled up and the air conditioning on, as the car's interior vibrated to the bass drum and guitar chords as *ACDC's "Highway to Hell"* lyrics flooded out of the speakers. It wouldn't be long now.

\*   \*   \*   \*   \*

Cameron parked in the parking lot across the street from the church. He opened his back door and retrieved from the garment hooks two sets of wardrobe hangers. One hanger held his rented tuxedo, and the other held his traditional Korean attire. In an effort to keep them from tangling and becoming wrinkled, he carried one set of clothes in each hand, slung over his shoulders. He definitely didn't want them dragging on the ground. As Cameron approached the sidewalk, it was difficult seeing cars coming in either direction. After allowing several cars to pass, Cameron entered the cross walk.

\*    \*    \*    \*    \*

Mike watched several cars pull into the church parking lot. He had parked close enough to have a good vantage point, but far enough away to avoid standing out. He continued waiting in his rental car, hoping to see Lee appear. He hadn't noticed another parking area located across the street until a man carrying several items slung over his shoulders stopped at the corner crosswalk, waiting for traffic to clear. Just at that moment, a horn rang out in the opposite direction. Mike turned toward the noise and saw that the driver of a new *Toyota Prius* had been waiting for a man to push a grocery cart full of recyclable containers across the street. The man jolted in surprise from the loud horn of the *Toyota* and appeared to pick up his pace as he continued to push his cart to the other side. Mike continued to watch until the Prius turned down the street and disappeared around the corner of the church.

\*    \*    \*    \*    \*

Cameron was halfway across the street when he heard the honking horn. As he proceeded across the street, he glanced up at an old man pushing a grocery cart. The driver must have grown impatient waiting for him. Cameron quickened his pace and bounced up the curb, then walked through the open side door to the church. As he entered the building, he could just hear the voice of the old man mumbling something as he continued to push his grocery cart across the street. Cameron continued into the church and walked toward the front office, where he would change his clothes and wait until the ceremony began. He glanced at the clock on the outside of the nave, where the wedding ceremony was to take place. It was 10:30 a.m. He still had plenty of time. Continuing down the hallway, Cameron saw the office. The priest waved him inside and closed the door behind him.

*    *    *    *    *

Mike turned back to the other side of the street and continued to look for Cameron. Because of the distraction earlier, he had forgotten about the man carrying the clothes hangers. Mike glanced at the clock mounted on the dashboard. It was 10:32 a.m. He knew the ceremony was scheduled to start at noon. He had ninety more minutes to find Lee. Mike continued to look up and down the street on both sides and could feel his patience begin to wane.

*    *    *    *    *

Reggie arrived early enough to stake out the area, but not too early where he would draw unwanted attention to himself. After glancing around the exterior of the church, Reggie pulled the black *Mercedes* into the parking lot behind the church. As he stepped out, he saw several Asian women who, based on their matching attire, must have been in the wedding party. Only one wasn't formally dressed. As she walked by the car, she seemed drawn to it. She stopped in her tracks. Standing on the sidewalk, she looked at the car. Her facial expression was one of shock. As Reggie opened the door and proceeded toward the front of the church, this same woman waited for him to approach. She walked up to Reggie, grabbed his wrist, and looked him in the face. Only then did she realize it wasn't who she thought it was.

With a sense of relief, she said "I'm sorry. I thought you were someone else. Your car reminded me of someone." She released his arm and joined her friends as she walked into the church. Reggie realized that the woman must have been Hye-Jin, the woman Jonathan had loved. The same woman he had been asked to protect. She was the reason he was there.

Reggie walked toward the front entrance. He could hear soft piano music and saw many guests standing in small groups outside. As he walked up the stairs and through the large doors, he could see through the interior doors of the nave. Just before the interior doors of the nave, there was a man dressed in a tuxedo standing near a small guest book table. As he approached the interior doors, the man spoke.

"Excuse me. Could you please sign the guest book?" he said with a smile. The man waited for a response as he pointed at the table that held the guest book. Reggie hadn't been invited. Not wanting to stand out, he did as he was told. Grabbing the pen, he looked down at the book. Underneath the heading title "Name", he wrote "On behalf of Jonathan." He left everything else blank and walked into the nave, where the ceremony was to be held. Looking around the elongated room, he saw a large cross mounted on the opposite wall. Reggie could see a lot of Asians sitting on the left side of the church. His assumption was correct that the groom's side would be sitting on the right side of the room. In order to avoid the possibility that someone would pursue a conversation with him, he searched for a section of pews containing the fewest people and sat there. As he looked up at the large cross at the front of the church, he began to think back to everything that had transpired and wondered how life had led him to this place in time. Holding the ceremony announcement, he began thinking back to the last conversation he'd had with Jonathan at the bar on their birthday.

\*     \*     \*     \*     \*

Reggie sat in his chair with a handful of peanuts, waiting to hear what Jonathan said next. Jonathan returned his mug of beer to the table and wiped his mouth on the sleeve of his button-down shirt.

"Yup. Crazy, huh? I've been thinking about that guy. If he's as crazy as his past makes him out to be, I certainly don't want him to know that I've been digging around his past, right?"

Reggie, having lived incarcerated for the last nine years, gave Jonathan a different point of view on things. It was quite different from the average household with a white picket fence and a pet dog. Reggie had grown up learning a different set of prison rules, where it was common knowledge that snitches, ex-cops, and pedophiles were fair game. In prison, even being caught talking behind someone's back had consequences. Such infractions outside of prison had zero consequences. But on the inside, it could mean being jumped. At worst, it meant getting stuck with a shank or even killed. With this type of experience, Reggie believed what Jonathan was suggesting made sense. With his eyes wide open, Reggie waited for Jonathan to explain what he had on his mind.

"The odds are a hundred to one that anything happens to me. But," pausing for effect, he looked down at Reggie before continuing, "I may need a favor from you."

Reggie nodded his head and replied, "What do you need done, Mr. Weed?" Reggie had an idea what he was about to ask, but he had learned years ago never to assume anything and never put words into someone else's mouth. He waited for Jonathan to reply.

"I doubt anything would happen to me, but if it did, I'm gonna have something sent to you." He took another drink from his beer before continuing. "I may need you to protect Hye-Jin. The only reason I would be out of the picture is if he wanted me out. Obviously, if I die from a cardiac arrest at a golf tournament or from a heart attack watching porn, that's a different situation," Jonathan joked and smiled before continuing. "But if I die from some strange-ass weird accident, one that sounds funny, makes you scratch your head, that's what I'm talking about." Jonathan finished off his beer. "I'm just saying, okay?" With that, Jonathan, stopped speaking and looked back at Reggie before feeling the urge to further explain his request. "Just keep in mind, Reg. If that happens, you've got to agree that he must be gunning for Hye-Jin and wanted me out of the way. He's already done it twice. Other than me and the investigator, no one else knows about this. If I can't protect her, who will?" Jonathan looked down at Reggie and waited for a reply. Without saying it, it was clear that Jonathan was asking much more from Reggie. He wanted Reggie to do more than protect her. If his fears came to fruition, he was asking Reggie to kill Cameron.

Reggie had been in this spot many times before. In the Youth Authority Detention Center, he had been one of the bigger guys there. When you combine that with his good behavior allowing him to stay until he maxed out on his twenty-first birthday, he was also one of the oldest inmates there. Most of the smaller guys had approached him, asking for similar protection. Only later had he learned that his street cred had been very high. It was well known that he had killed a grown man with his bare hands. To be able to share that Reggie had promised retribution against anyone who hurt one of the smaller guys had been enough to protect them during their stay.

Jonathan's request would have made a normal person more than uncomfortable. Not Reggie. He'd done it in the past. He couldn't imagine why he wouldn't agree. Up until now, nothing had happened. He hadn't had to keep his word. Hoping this would be the same, Reggie replied, "Yes sir, Mr. Weed. I'll take care of it."

Jonathan looked at Reggie. He could tell that this kid was all business. During Jonathan's business life, he had finalized countless deals. He had become a good judge of person's character. He believed Reggie.

"Thanks, man. I appreciate it. I'll write it up first thing before I take her out on the big date. Let me see your license one more time," Jonathan asked Reggie.

Not knowing why he needed it, Reggie reached into his wallet, grabbed his ID, and handed it to Jonathan. "Is everything current, address and everything?" he asked Reggie.

"Yes sir, but it's only an ID. I don't drive, Mr. Weed. Is that okay?" Reggie asked.

"Oh yeah, it's fine," replied Jonathan. He then reached into his wool jacket breast pocket, removed his smart phone and snapped a picture of the ID before giving it back to Reggie. "In my world, Reggie," continued Jonathan, "when you strike a deal, you never procrastinate. I learned that one a long time ago. Once it's agreed, get the contract written up and signed before someone changes their mind." In an overdramatic fashion, Jonathan explained "I'll have my guy write it up." Glancing up at the clock, he began to stand, extended his right hand toward Reggie, and said, "If you don't put it in writing, it never happened." After a brief pause, Jonathan continued. "Seriously, with all my heart, I truly appreciate you taking me seriously and for helping me out. If something were to happen that is," said Jonathan.

"Yes sir, Mr. Weed. I'll take care of it," Reggie replied. As he watched Jonathan walking to the door, he asked, "Are you sure you're okay to drive?" Looking back over his shoulder, he yelled, "I'm good to go, my friend. And, oh yeah: Happy birthday to us, right?" With that, he turned and walked out of the bar.

\*  \*  \*  \*  \*

Reggie continued reading the wedding announcement and ceremony schedule that he'd been given after signing the guest book. The paper quality reminded him of the document he had signed at the attorney's office. He remembered when he had arrived at the soup kitchen two weeks after the birthday celebration he had with Jonathan at the bar. Reggie was curious, wondering where Mr. Weed was. He hadn't seen him since he had arrived. He was surprised when one of Jonathan's friends, another volunteer, approached him with the sad news that Jonathan had died. He was told the basic facts about the boating accident and that was it. Reggie couldn't help but think back to their discussion at the bar. As he was lost in his thoughts, one of Jonathan's other friends, an attorney, approached Reggie.

The attorney had already told the other volunteers about Jonathan and found out that Reggie had just learned what happened. Reggie was in shock as the attorney asked him to accompany him back to his office off of Olympic Boulevard. He told Reggie he had spoken to Jonathan the day after their birthday celebration, and that Mr. Weed had changed his will and included Reginald Chambers as one of his beneficiaries. The attorney checked Reggie's ID against the photograph that Jonathan had provided him. It was a perfect match. The attorney then read a statement to Reggie, which detailed what he had been gifted: a black *Mercedes* automobile; a $20,000 prepaid credit card intended for gas, insurance, and vehicle registration; and a five-year prepaid maintenance agreement.

"The current insurance and vehicle registration are in the glove box. I understand you don't have your driver license yet, so we've made arrangements for the vehicle to be held in storage until you pass your driver's test. At that point, we'll have the vehicle delivered to you. This was part of the contingency he set up. He knows your parole situation and doesn't want to put you in a situation that could get you in trouble by driving without a driver's license," the attorney explained.

The attorney explained that Jonathan didn't want the expenses for the vehicle to become a burden. Finally, the attorney slid Reggie a one-hundred-thousand-dollar cashier's check with a note in a sealed envelope. The letter was to remain sealed, intended for Reggie's eyes only.

Reggie was instructed to unseal the envelope and read the note to himself but not aloud. Once he did that, he handed the letter back to the attorney, who placed it in his high-speed shredder. Reggie then was handed a thick manila envelope, which he later discovered contained the evidence Jonathan had uncovered on Cameron Sivesind. After a Notary Public was brought into the room, Reggie signed a full release confirming that he had received everything he was entitled to receive, based on Jonathan Weed's last will and testament. The document was notarized and photocopied, and the copy was given to Reggie.

"I'm sorry for your loss, Reggie. Do you have any questions for me?" the attorney asked.

"Just one," Reggie replied. How did Mr. Weed die?"

"It was an unfortunate accident," replied the attorney. "He had been thrown from a boat he was piloting. The police believe he was knocked out after he drove too close to the shoreline. They think his head struck a tree limb, causing him to hit his head on the side of the boat as he fell into the water and later drown in the lake."

"That's unusual, isn't it?" asked Reggie.

"Very. I've been doing this twenty years. It's the first time I've had one of my clients pass away under such strange circumstances."

That's all Reggie had to know. He nodded his head, letting it all sink in.

# 19

Mike continued to watch for Cameron's arrival. But based on the number of cars arriving, there was a strong possibility he had missed him. Mike had been sitting in his rental car and had finished drinking the Big Gulp soda he'd picked up on his way to the church. The drink was having its effect, and he was starting to feel uncomfortable. He needed to go to the restroom. He couldn't wait any longer and was just about to open his car door when he saw a group of women waiting near the side entrance to the church. All but one had been wearing matching formal dresses. The woman in casual attire stood in contrast from the rest. Mike assumed they all must be part of the wedding party.

Mike focused on the casually dressed woman and couldn't miss her big smile, beaming with excitement. He was certain she was Hye-Jin Kim, the bride, and her enthusiasm was contagious. Mike began to feel a sense of elation as he watched her about to begin the next phase of her life. As he continued to watch, a deep sense of sadness gripped him. At that moment, he began to think back to his sister's wedding day and how she also had been full of excitement and anticipation. Mike's thoughts were interrupted as he saw her stop on the sidewalk as if waiting for someone in the parking lot. At first, Mike thought it might be Lee, but the man who approached her was much taller and younger. He continued watching until the woman and the young man walked in separate entrances into the church.

His full bladder could no longer be ignored. Mike exited his rental car and scurried across the street. As he entered the church, he saw an arrow sign directing him to the restrooms. He avoided the group of people who were gathered near a small table, apparently waiting to sign something. As he continued down the hallway, he could hear the piano music spilling through an open side door. Glancing inside, he could see that many people were already sitting in the pews. He continued walking down the hallway, where he saw the men's restroom door. He quickened his pace. With a sense of urgency, he pushed through the restroom door and made a beeline to the first available urinal.

\* \* \* \* \*

Cameron sat in the office waiting. He glanced at his watch. He still had twenty minutes. He had drunk way to much water while he waited and had already visited the restroom twice. The excitement contributed to his condition, and he told the priest who was waiting with him that he needed to go one more time. With a smile, the priest said that was normal. Cameron opened the door and made his way to the restroom.

As Cameron stepped inside, he noticed a man using one of the urinals. He walked up to the only other one available, right next to him.

\* \* \* \* \*

Reggie looked up at the wall clock. The ceremony was set to start in a little over fifteen minutes. As he waited, he had been thinking about everything—his past and all of the things he'd done to bring him to this point. He regretted making that promise to Jonathan. He began to feel obligated to keep his word. He had received the car, the money, the credit card, everything. For months, he had contemplating what he would do. He had decided that only if the opportunity presented itself would he do it here, now, before the wedding. He knew that if he missed doing it today, he would have many more other opportunities in the future. Reggie glanced around the room. The church was filling up with guests. He glanced toward the front of the church and couldn't miss the large cross mounted on the wall. He stared at it as if asking for divine intervention. With a sudden sense of confidence, Reggie stood up and began to maneuver around other guests to exit the row. After making it to the main aisle, he began walking toward the front of the church and into the lobby. He approached the same man he met earlier in front of the guest book and spoke.

"Where is the reception being held?" Reggie asked. "Is that where we should take presents?"

"It's just down the street. The address is listed on the ceremony schedule," the man replied as he pointed to the thick pink paper Reggie was holding in his hand. Looking into the man's eyes, Reggie began sizing him up. It was an automatic reflex, something he'd developed from the years of being incarcerated. Habits were hard to break.

# 20

Hye-Jin was lying on her bed, waiting for her restaurant manager to pick her up. She had already changed into the same clothes she had worn when she first walked into the hospital eighteen months ago. On that day, the same restaurant manager had dropped her off. At that very moment, he was on his way to pick her up, fighting the rush-hour traffic that, like clockwork, began around 2:30 every weekday. The traffic became increasingly more congested until most freeways throughout Los Angeles County were reduced to a virtual crawl. She was grateful to have this manager. She trusted him, and he knew everyone on her staff very well. He had been taking care of everything since her hospitalization.

Until she had made the decision to come to the mental hospital, she hadn't considered how long it had been since she'd had a vacation. Ever since she had arrived in the US, she'd been on the go. With her head down, and a full head of steam, she began chasing the American dream. She'd been on that track every day, never even considering getting off of the track.

Every now and then, she would just think about visiting her parents back in Seoul. However, because she had broken off the engagement, she knew that she was the reason her family had lost face with the other business families back in Korea. Hye-Jin's departure was her way of apologizing to her family. It would now be up to her younger brother to uphold their family name. After her grandfather had passed away twenty-two years prior, it had become easier for her to forget her past life. For all intents and purposes, Hye-Jin had been informally disowned. She never called or wrote. Her parents hadn't even known that she had been engaged to be married here in the US. It had been so long ago since she had last spoken to them.

Coming here after the wedding debacle was a great escape. It gave her time to revisit her past and come to grips with her real isolation. Thankfully, her business kept her surrounded by people and gave her life purpose. However, so many things had come to a sudden, unexpected halt. It was the unanticipated finality with which she lost things that day, a day that had brought so much promise. It was that deep contrast of expectations and emotions that had pushed her over the edge.

The events that took place that day came as such a shock that she needed and wanted a place to hide. It was just too much for her to process. The last eighteen months had done the trick. As she waited for the custodian to bring in her last cup of tea, she took off her shoes, tucked her hands under her head, and lay down, stretching out on her bed. As she began to relax, she thought back to that day. It was the day that started out so wonderfully, a day she believed had so much promise. She had looked forward to being married to a man she had loved with all of her heart and soul. Even now, even after she had read all of the contents in that envelope about his past life, even after speaking to the private investigator who had uncovered everything, she found it difficult to believe. Until then, she thought she was a good judge of character. She believed that what was shared between her and Cameron was mutual and much more than just an attraction. It was like the reunion of lost soul mates. In her eyes, in her mind, it was all real. Cameron had never asked her about her finances. He didn't need money. Their love was real.

Hye-Jin glanced over at her *Country Jasmines*. They had been delivered two days prior. She had arranged for them to be delivered twice a week. This was the last bouquet she would receive at this place. As her mind began to drift, she glanced out the industrial-strength, metal-screen-covered open window. She could feel the gentle breeze drift into her space with the unique aroma of her favorite floral scent. Her mind continued drifting back to her wedding day.

* * * * *

She couldn't remember smiling so much. She was bubbling over with excitement. She had been laughing all day, looking forward to the marriage ceremony. She couldn't wait for Cameron to see her in her white *Vera Wang* gown. She had purchased it at the Rodeo Drive store. Her friends came during the fitting. They had made a day of it. They ate lunch afterward, and Hye-Jin treated all of her brides maids to a two-hour full body massage back in K-town. She had just completed her make up and put on her wedding gown. They were admiring how beautiful she looked when they heard a commotion coming from inside the church. One of her bridesmaids went out to see what had happened. When she returned to the room, everyone could see from her facial expression that something was seriously wrong.

"Hye-Jin, something's happened to Cameron. You need to come right away!"

Hye-Jin stood and began walking toward the nave of the church where the guests were waiting for the ceremony to begin. As she entered the lobby, she heard an unexpected noise as the front doors to the church were forced open. She glanced back and could see a large man pushing against them and walking through, exiting the building. She paused and thought that it was the same man that she had mistaken for Jonathan, realizing later that it was the black *Mercedes* that had caused the confusion. It was the same model that Jonathan had owned.

Hye-Jin continued toward the entrance to the nave. She paused just outside, knowing that she had been instructed to enter this archway after hearing the *Wedding March* song. The same bridesmaid that had made the discovery saw Hye-Jin pause and took the initiative. She could sense her reluctance to walk into the room before it was time. She grabbed Hye-Jin's hand and walked ahead of her.

"Come on, you need to get back to the side hallway," she said, looking into Hye-Jin's face. As they entered the nave, she could hear the murmurings of several whispered conversations suddenly stop. It was followed by gasps of disbelief as many of the women guests began commenting on how beautiful she looked. But there was something in the tone of their voices. The emotional content was wrong. It sounded like disbelief and sadness, as opposed to one of excitement and exhilaration. Hye-Jin could hear the subtle distinction and knew that something terrible must have happened. As she increased her pace, she could see a crowd of people in the hallway through the open side doors. As she walked past the last pew, she saw a man seated there who seemed to be frozen in shock, and his face was ashen. He avoided making eye contact. She didn't recognize him and kept running toward the hallway. It was Mike.

Picking up the hem of her long wedding dress, she began running at full sprint toward the hallway. She could see one of the groomsmen performing CPR on Cameron. The priest saw Hye-Jin and ran toward her.

"I was going into the restroom to check on him. I found him passed out on his back. It looks like he slipped and hit his head," explained the priest. "He's not breathing. We've already called 911. An ambulance is on its way. They are just down the street. They should be here any minute."

While two men switched off and continued to administer CPR, Hye-Jin knelt down by Cameron's side and held his hand. After several minutes, one man yelled out, "He's breathing!"

With a flash of hope, Hye-Jin squeezed Cameron's hand and continued to wait. In the distance, she could hear the siren becoming progressively louder. Some of the guests yelled out, "I can hear it. It's almost here!" Hye-Jin placed Cameron's hand between both of hers, then leaned down and kissed the back of his hand. She stroked the hair off of his forehead as she heard the side entrance to the church fly open with two paramedics pushing a gurney through the narrow hallway. One of the paramedics leaned down, checking Cameron's pulse by touching his neck. Looking at his partner, he said "It's very weak. Let's get him up and on the way to *Cedars-Sinai*."

As the two paramedics picked up Cameron, Hye-Jin got her first look at the back of his head. There was a large area of his skull that must have hit the hard tile floor. The back of his head had been bleeding. His hair was matted and sticky from the large amount of blood that had pooled. Several large gasps came from the guests as they saw his injuries. Hye-Jin held onto Cameron's hand and followed him into the back of the open ambulance doors. With help from a crew of firefighters who had arrived on the scene, she climbed into the ambulance. The frightened priest stood outside of the ambulance doors, holding both his hands in front of his chest, and his face flinched from the sound of the ambulance doors slamming shut just before the siren started up, echoing as it drove away through the busy street. The sound of the sirens faded somewhat as the ambulance made its way toward *Cedars-Sinai Medical Center*, ten blocks away.

The church was full of guests. It was eerily quiet. No one knew what to say or do. As the priest came back into the nave, everyone looked up at him for an update on what had happened. Taking a deep breath, the priest was about to speak when the church bells began to sound out. Everyone seemed to realize the irony of the moment. It was twelve noon. The wedding ceremony was scheduled to begin at that very moment. The emotional turmoil was just too much, and many of the guests began to cry. The priest waited for the last bell to chime. He wanted to make sure that everyone would be able to hear what he was about to say.

*   *   *   *   *

Hye-Jin had pushed her white wedding dress down out of the way so the paramedics could continue to work on Cameron. The ambulance continued to speed down Wilshire Boulevard, nearing their destination. She leaned her face down inches from Cameron's cheek, while she squeezed his hand. As the paramedics finished installing his IV, oxygen nose fitting, and EKG hook ups, they busied themselves completing his chart notes so they could report all of their emergency procedures to the ER nurses. For a brief moment, Cameron awoke. With a huge sense of relief, Hye-Jin smiled for the first time since she had stepped out of the church dressing room. She leaned down and kissed his cheek.

"Are you okay? I was so worried, Cam." Tears of joy and fear pooled within Hye-Jin's eyes. Remaining strong, she blinked back her tears. She could see that he was trying to speak. She tilted her head so her ear was directly over his mouth. Cameron blinked his eyes, trying to focus. He was so grateful to see Hye-Jin. He could feel a sense of urgency within his body, his mind, his soul. So many people contemplate what their last words will be. Not knowing when, or who would be in your presence, makes it that much more difficult to imagine. But for Cameron, it couldn't have ended any better. He had found the woman of his dreams. He had changed. He had burned his safety net and returned most of his unworthy spoils of greed to one of its rightful owners. He had somehow changed. His life, and now his soul, had a chance. He yearned to say his final good-byes. In a whisper, Cameron spoke.

"I'm so sorry to leave you like this. You are the only good thing I have ever been a part of. I love you with everything that I am and ever will be. I will love you forever." Cameron's voice trailed off. In his last breath he whispered, "Don't forget me."

Hye-Jin could feel his last breath push back the hair that hung across her ear. She could feel his hand relax between hers. She tilted her head and looked into his eyes. She could see the last glimmer of sparkle in his eyes fade away just before he closed his eyes. Before the heart monitor rang out its unmistakable flat-line screech, Hye-Jin knew. She pressed her soft lips against his mouth one last time as she kissed him good-bye.

Anticipating the sound, she leaned back to give the paramedics room to perform their duties: CPR and then the defibrillator. Outwardly, she showed appreciation for their efforts with the hope that he would be saved. But inside, she knew he was gone.

They continued to work on Cameron's body as they pulled into the emergency room. The back doors of the ambulance flew open before the vehicle had come to a complete stop. The paramedics unfolded the wheels on the gurney in one smooth motion and rolled him into the ER. Hye-Jin gathered herself. Unassisted, she climbed out of the back of the ambulance. As she walked toward the back door, the sensors detected her presence. The ER staff froze in awe as she walked through the doors. With the bright sunlight shining through the doors, the glare seemed to add to the effect it had on her image as she entered the room. Her beautiful white flowing gown seemed surreal in the chaotic environment of the hospital ER. It was as if an angel had just walked in. Hye-Jin proceeded toward the closest seat where she sat down, cradled her head in her hands, and began crying.

# 21

**A** custodian walked into Hye-Jin's room, carrying a cup of hot tea. It had become a nightly ritual after dinner but before bedtime. "Excuse me, Miss Kim. I heard today's your last with us. Is that right?" the custodian asked.

"Yes. I'm on my way around six. I wanted my last cup of tea before I go. Besides, I think my ride is stuck in traffic," said Hye-Jin, as she looked at the custodian while relaxing on her bed. "If you could put it on the end table near my flowers, that would be great."

The custodian carried the cup to the end table. As she prepared to set the cup down on the nightstand, her intercom phone squawked and distracted her, and she misjudged the distance. Consequently, as she released the cup, it was too close to the vase and she bumped the side. This slight jolt caused a vibration that resonated throughout the vessel. The water inside accentuated the vibration still further. This small, seemingly insignificant shockwave caused the flower stems to shake; and this extra movement, combined with the soft breeze that had been entering through the window, further accentuated the chain reaction. Each new drift of air seemed to catch the petals like small parachutes, pulling the petals and tearing their connecting fibers away from the stem. Over time, the fiber endings that had kept them attached to the center of the flower weakened. The next ocean breeze blew through the open window, and the stress that had been placed on the petals reached the breaking point. This chain reaction, one that had been taking place since the flowers had arrived, had finally taken its toll. In that instant, several large petals began to break away from the main stem, and each petal that broke free began to drift downward.

Life's circumstances sometimes seem random. One could argue that this was one of those times. If the cup had been placed another inch in either direction, the petals would have bounced off its rim, continuing to drift away and fall to the floor. But that isn't what happened.

As Hye-Jin smiled up at the custodian, she didn't notice several of the petals falling into her cup of tea. The soft, thin spongy petals floated on the surface of the liquid until they began to absorb the moisture in the tea. As each second passed, they became more saturated. In what seemed like no time at all, the excess weight of the petals caused them to sink to the bottom of the cup, where they began to disintegrate and dissolve. If the cup had contained another type of clear liquid, Hye-Jin might have noticed. But she liked her tea strong. She waved good-bye to the custodian, who was walking out the door. "Thank you."

The custodian turned around and gave Hye-Jin a brief but sincere smile. "You're welcome, Miss Kim. Honestly, it was a pleasure. I wish you all the best." Then she left the room. Hye-Jin remained lying on the bed and closed her eyes, enjoying the soft ocean breeze as she waited for her manager to arrive. She closed her eyes and began to doze off. While she slept, more petals fell into her cup.

*    *    *    *    *

Greg's first day as an intern was coming to an end. It was much better than he had expected. He'd worried that the patients would be out of control, or he would be fearful for his safety. All his fears were laid to rest, and he looked forward to this new opportunity. As he prepared to leave for the day, he received a call on his cellphone. Seeing his mother's number flash on the screen got his attention. She rarely called.

"Mom," Greg said as he answered the phone.

"Greg, dear, your sister went into labor sooner than we anticipated. We're all down at the hospital now. We wanted to wait before calling everyone in case it was a false alarm. But it's the real deal!" His mother was hurried and clearly excited. This baby was going to be her first grandchild.

"Awesome!" replied Greg. "Is she doing okay? No complications?"

"None; she's doing fine. The baby is ready a little sooner than the doctor had expected. Will you be able to get down here in time, dear?"

"I was just about ready to leave," Greg said. "Let me grab my stuff and I'll be on my way. Hopefully, the traffic has calmed down a little. It'll take me about forty minutes. I'll see everybody soon." After concluding the call, Greg went straight to the locker room, changed into his street clothes, and punched out his timecard. As he walked toward the elevator, he glanced into Miss Kim's room. He saw her relaxing on her bed with her eyes closed.

*    *    *    *    *

The elevator bell woke Hye-Jin from her nap. She stretched her arms and opened her mouth with a big yawn. As she became more awake, she glanced toward the window and saw her cup of tea. She glanced at the wire-encased clock mounted on the wall. It was almost six. She stood, walked over to the end table, and picked up her tea. As she raised the cup to her mouth, she noticed a strong aroma. She paused and looked down toward the vase of *Country Jasmine* flowers. In a daze, still sleepy from her nap, she carried the cup back to her bed and sat down. Holding the cup and looking out the window, she was reminded of that evening, the day she was to have married. Her thoughts drifted back to that night, waiting by herself, looking out on the night lights and passing cars along Wilshire Boulevard. It was here that she learned the truth. It had all happened at the reception hall.

*    *    *    *    *

Her restaurant manager had stayed with her at Cedars-Sinai. Cameron had been declared dead at 12:34 p.m. The manager had provided the hospital with all of Hye-Jin's contact information. He had made the necessary arrangements so she wouldn't be burdened with the details. As they drove back to the restaurant, he had one more stop to make. He had to make sure that the reception hall and other vendors were paid. He had notified the hall manager of what had happened. Nothing needed to be said, he understood that everyone still expected to be paid; the hall had been booked well in advance, the caterer had prepared the cake and food; the band was booked and ready to perform; and the photographer had his cameras ready. Before he drove to the hospital to pick up Hye-Jin, he had already placed a call confirming he would be there to settle up with everyone. He had instructed the caterer to donate the food to a local shelter of his choice.

Hye-Jin's restaurant manager parked his car in front of the hall. He urged her to remain in the car. She refused and explained she just didn't want to be alone. He walked around the car and opened the door. As she stepped out, her wedding dress sprang and draped out, hanging perfectly and hovering just above the ground. She had never put her veil on. It must still be back at the church. The hall manager looked out of the large plate glass windows into the dusk night. The beautiful colors of the setting sun against the clouds made a perfect backdrop as Miss Kim and her tuxedo-clad restaurant manager approached the doors.

Her manager couldn't help but feel the disappointment and sadness of that day. A wedding celebration is one of the most cherished occasions in a woman's life: The planning of every detail. The hours of thought that go into each decision. The sheer number of people involved to put on such an event. The cumulative effort of all the participants, striving to do their best, creates its own energy. It's a beautiful, unique experience that is shared by everyone involved. The sudden unexpected cancellation was difficult for everyone. All of them, in their own way, had suffered a loss, but no more so than the one person who had been the ultimate decision maker for everything—the bride. The burden and tragic loss of her husband-to-be; the disappointing cancellation of the ceremony and all of the tasks that were to be performed, food, cake, band, photos, the things that would not be enjoyed—it was the bride who carried the weight of that loss.

The hall manager stood inside the front door as the pair walked in. He couldn't find the courage to look either of them in the eye. With his head tilted in a frozen perpetual bow, he waited for them to speak. He didn't know what to say. Words had escaped him.

The restaurant manager walked up to the hall manager and in a whispered voice spoke.

"Thank you so much for all of your efforts. We all were looking forward to enjoying everything you had planned. It is with great sadness that we come together now like this," he said as he bowed his head.

Hye-Jin's restaurant manager had been carrying a duffle bag that he now placed on the table. He looked up and saw that the hall had been cleaned. They knew that Miss Kim was on her way down, and no one wanted her to see the flowers, tables, and decorations. The restaurant manager scanned the room and again bowed his head toward the hall manager, acknowledging the effort it must have taken to clear everything in such a short time. After making eye contact, he said, "*Kamsahamnida*" ("Thank you").

The hall manager bowed back and replied, "You're welcome." He then paused and leaned forward so that Miss Kim couldn't hear. "There's another matter I need to discuss."

Assuming he was referring to the money to pay the vendors, the restaurant manager pointed at the black duffle bag. Realizing the misunderstanding, the hall manager replied, "No, no. that can wait. We can resolve that later." Leaning in closer, he continued, "We didn't know what to do with the presents. We've stacked them in the back room." As he finished speaking, he raised his eyebrows and with a quick upward tilt of his chin, he pointed toward the back doorway in the back of the hall.

Contemplating what to do, the restaurant manager raised his hand to his face, rubbed his chin and exhaled a deep sigh as he considered how to proceed. The hall manager pulled an envelope off of the table and handed it to him and explained, "This plain postage envelope had been hand-delivered here by a tall young *mi-gook saram* (American) around noon today. It wasn't wrapped in wrapping paper." They each stared at the package. On the top, handwritten in a black ink pen, were the words "FOR HYE-JIN KIM ONLY."

Hye-Jin remained seated on one of the chairs closest to the large plate glass window. She stared out onto busy Wilshire Blvd. The street lights had come on, and the other bright, colorful street signs and the headlights of the passing cars were mesmerizing. She sat alone, watching the outside activity. She was still in shock.

Both managers walked to the back room. As the hall manager opened the door, Hye-Jin's restaurant manager saw all of the presents, wrapped in beautiful colors and bows, stacked up one on top of the other. There were one hundred fifty-two packages. The hall manager had instructed his workers to count each one. They had also prepared a list of the guests' names that had been written on the gift tags. The only one that was unaccounted for was the large plain envelope that the restaurant manager held in his hand.

The restaurant manager knew what he had to do. It wasn't his place to decide for Miss Kim. Before he went back outside, he sat the duffle bag on the table and reached inside. He pulled out the envelopes and handed them to the hall manager. It was customary for the hall manager to act as the bride's contact for all the other vendors. With a deep bow, the hall manager accepted the envelopes and walked them to the back office, where he locked them in the safe. It was understood by both men that this quick transaction held a dangerous element. In their community, it was also an unspoken understanding that each manager would be carrying a pistol. The protection wasn't needed for the involved parties, but for others who may foolishly attempt to prey on others. However, during the most recent riots in Los Angeles, the rest of the world had learned that the Korean community, as a whole, understood their place in the community. They appreciated the fact that they represented a disproportionate number of business owners. As a result, many thieves had learned the hard way that members of this community took everything seriously and they came prepared. The world had witnessed firsthand those images that had been blasted out over many of the television networks, demonstrating the resolve, courage, and loyalty these people possessed as they held off would-be looters with shotguns and handguns from the roof tops of their small businesses. They were a force to be reckoned with and never to be taken lightly.

The restaurant manager contemplated how to proceed. Miss Kim was his superior and owned the business. She had selected him as someone she could trust and count on. At the same time, he was human, and he appreciated the timing of such matters. He accepted the position and understood the responsibility he had been given. He had a duty to keep her abreast of everything. If he delayed presenting the envelope to her on the assumption that it could wait, although understandable and reasonable under the circumstances, the contents could also be very important. They could pertain to something that he was not privy to. Contemplating further, the package didn't seem to have anything to do with the wedding. It seemed to be a matter unrelated to the ceremony. As such, he concluded that it wasn't his place to decide. She was his superior and she was his employer.

Knowing what he had to do, he carried the envelope to Miss Kim. As he walked toward her, he could feel the sense of dread with every step he took. He gathered as much courage and strength as he could find before he spoke. With a bowed head, avoiding eye contact, he spoke.

"Excuse me, Miss Kim. At this moment, I would prefer not to bring this matter to your attention. But it is not my place to decide. A package was delivered here today at noon. The hall manager didn't know if it belonged with the other wedding presents. Based on the packaging, it doesn't appear to be. I didn't know the importance of its contents and felt compelled to bring it to your attention." Still bowing at the waist, the restaurant manager handed Hye-Jin the envelope.

*     *     *     *     *

Greg arrived at the *UC Irvine Medical Center*, parked his car, and made his way to the maternity ward. He had kept the cellphone on speaker during an on-going conversation with his mother throughout the entire drive to the hospital. His battery was running very low. Everything was fine, and his sister had been taken into the delivery room. His brother-in-law was nervous and was forbidden from taking videos or photographs. His sister didn't want anything documenting her naked swollen belly or contorted face for the entire world to see. Everyone in the waiting room was in high spirits as Greg walked through the doors. He exchanged hugs and distributed cigars. He had been carrying them for weeks. He couldn't wait to pass them out. He wasn't sure about the etiquette, so he had one for each person, not just the guys.

\*   \*   \*   \*   \*

Hye-Jin stared at the plain *US Postal Service* oversized envelope package. For a brief moment, she reverted back to her business mindset. She studied the packing, contemplating if she had expected anything. As her mind raced through her current dealings, she seemed confident that it wasn't business related. Yet the packaging didn't suggest that it was a wedding present, either.

The hall manager, from the safety of his office, watched the scene unfold on his security cameras. It was uncanny. Watching Miss Kim, dressed in a wedding gown, sitting alone in the empty banquet hall that she had rented for that evening, opening a plainly wrapped envelope before any of the other gorgeously wrapped presents. It was as if that moment represented a tale of opposites.

As she pulled back the perforated tab, she found a manila file envelope full of loose papers, newspaper articles and photograph clippings. As she tilted the postal envelope on its side, attempting to dump out the contents, a sealed letter slid out, tumbling onto the table. As she read the writing on the envelope, she dropped the postal envelope in shock and raised both of her hands and cradled her face. She had recognized the handwriting. He had a draftsman style of penmanship. He printed everything in capital letters and her name was written on the small envelope. It was from Jonathan. He was the last person she would have guessed; he was dead.

To receive that package today, on the day that she was supposed to marry; she had to know what this was all about. Contemplating this ironic set of circumstances, Hye-Jin found a renewed source of energy. Having something else to think about other than today's events would be a welcome distraction. Or so she thought.

She tore off the short side of the envelope and threw the scrap onto the table. Then she squeezed the envelope. As it opened, she reached inside and pulled out the note and began reading.

Hye-Jin,

If you are reading this note, then something must have happened to me. I am most likely dead, caused by a strange accident. I have no way of protecting you now. So if this did happen to me, I've asked a friend to take care of you and protect you. I've asked him to make sure you see everything I found out about Cameron Sivesind. It's all in this package. Whatever you do, don't trust him. He is not who you think he is. He changed his name. He was married two times before. And both of his wives are dead. You can't trust him.

Please read everything I've provided. Contact the investigator I hired. His information is inside. There is nothing else I can do. I love you.

Sincerely and with all my heart,
Jonathan Weed

The restaurant manager stood watching for Miss Kim's reaction. The hall manager also watched through the security camera. Hye-Jin appeared to have read the note. She placed it on the table. She betrayed no reaction--not sadness, not anger. She pursed her lips and stood from the table. She placed her hands on her hips and stared out the large plate glass windows. She took several deep breaths and watched the reflection of the lights and the passing cars dance around like a disco ball. Without warning, Hye-Jin dropped her arms to her sides and bent her legs as if she were about to make a broad-jump leap across a narrow stream full of water. As her legs extended upward into a full stretch, her face contorted as she released a guttural scream of agony that reverberated throughout the banquet hall. The veins and tendons in her neck stood out as her face shook. With her mouth gaping open, she released all of the pain, frustration, anger, and now hatred, all at once. Her mind was unable to deal with the onslaught of conflicting feelings. Her voice began to crack as her vocal cords reached their breaking point, her eyes rolled back into her head, and she collapsed.

# 22

Hye-Jin blinked her eyes. She had been stuck between worlds. Her mind had been frozen. She couldn't move on. She didn't know what to believe. She didn't know what to do. Her heart had told her that Jonathan was wrong. Cameron wasn't like that. But how could she ignore the newspaper articles, or, the fact that he had changed his name and had kept it all a secret? He'd never told her anything. Why?

She reasoned that if he had told her, what would she have thought? If she were honest with herself, she knew he had been right not to have told her. She would have run straight for the hills and never looked back. She knew that to be true. So, was Jonathan right? Was everything she experienced with Cameron a setup? Was he just acting? Her mind said yes, but her heart and her soul said otherwise.

Those inconsistencies had set her mind on a constant mental loop. She would replay all of the facts in her mind, and then mentally counter those arguments with her intuition and feelings. It was a never-ending mental gymnastics match that had no winner. Both sides were right and wrong at the same time. But now, her rational mind had made peace with the subconscious self. Regardless of the answer, they were now both gone. She had spent enough time. She had wasted enough energy. If her grandfather were able to give advice, he would have told her that she had spent too much of her valuable sand from her precious hourglass. He would remind her that life was supposed to be lived. As he had done in the past, he would emphasize that everyone is given a certain amount of time on this earth. It could end unexpectedly and without warning. We must each live our lives to the fullest. We must not waste a single grain of sand that has been allocated to our personal hourglass.

Hye-Jin looked up at the clock. It was a quarter past six. She glanced up and thought she heard her restaurant manager's voice. Feeling a new sense of urgency, a new sense of purpose, she walked over to the window, looked at her flowers holding her now-cold cup of tea. With a quick flip of her wrist and as she tilted her head back, she drank the entire cup. As she placed the cup back on the table, she noticed that the tea seemed stronger than usual, with a bitter taste. She wiped her mouth on her sleeve and walked out to meet her manager. She was excited to see him again after all this time. She had instructed him not to visit her or tell anyone where she was. He had told everyone that she had gone back to Korea for a break.

As she approached her manager, she did something that she never did. She opened her arms, giving him a large hug. They both smiled and laughed. As they walked toward the elevator, one of the nurses asked, "What should we do with your paintings?"

As she reached the elevator, she looked back and replied, *"Mola!"* ("I don't know!") "It's up to you. You can keep them if you want. Or just throw them away. As the elevator doors began closing, Hye-Jin looked at her restaurant manager and said, "All of a sudden I'm very sleepy."

*　*　*　*　*

Greg and his family had waited only fifteen minutes before his sister had delivered her baby. It was a healthy girl. They had already decided beforehand to name her Dominique. Being the first grandchild, it was a perfect name. She would be treated as a special jewel.

All of Greg's family waited outside the maternity ward viewing windows. As his brother-in-law stepped through the door with the nurse carrying the tiny bundle, everyone let out a communal gasp of joy and excitement, accompanied by smiles, laughter, and tears of joy. The newest addition to the family had entered the world. The nurse and Greg's brother-in-law, in their surgical-mask-covered faces, walked up inches away from the glass window, giving everyone a closer look. Even with the mask, one could sense his huge smile of joy and relief at having gotten through the delivery unscathed. It was like a scene from an Academy Awards ceremony as famous actors posed for photographs. The reflection in the glass window that separated the newborn from the well-intended hoard of onlookers was a sight to see. After several moments, the nurse placed the baby in a bassinette between two other baby boys that had been born earlier that day. The nurse bent down into Dominique's crib and inserted a pink card with her mother's name written on it. She slid it into the acrylic slot that was situated in the upper portion of the crib. The nurse then double-checked the baby's wristband, confirming that it matched the card information. This was a standard procedure to assure that no babies would become switched by accident. The names and ID numbers were a perfect match. The nurse then walked the new father out of the nursery, allowing little Dominique time to recover and rest with the other newborns.

Each family member took turns taking photographs. The newborn babies were oblivious to their stardom as they slept, recovering from their challenging ordeals. Greg waited his turn, knowing that the grandparents had earned the right to this special occasion. As the grandparents and aunts stepped away from the window, Greg raised his cellphone camera and snapped a picture of all the newborns lined up in a row with their scrunched faces fast asleep. As he looked down to check the quality of the picture, making sure that it was clear and not blurred, his phone battery died. Before he could view the photo, his phone shut down. He reached into his pocket for the charger cord he habitually carried in his jacket pocket and realized that in his rush to leave work, he had left it in his locker.

Greg mingled with his extended family, going back several more times to the window to see the baby. As the level of excitement subsided, everyone began to feel comfortable to let the mother and newborn rest. It had been an emotional and exhausting event, leaving many of them tired and in need of sleep, themselves. After Greg made his last rounds of hugs, kisses, and congratulatory exchanges, he walked back to his car. He decided he needed to go back to Long Beach and get his cellphone wall charger. He jumped into his car and drove back to the 405. The traffic had eased and was moving quickly. It would take him only fifteen minutes to get there.

\*     \*     \*     \*     \*

Reggie was sitting in the showroom at the car dealership, staring at the newest *Dodge Charger* on display. He had already cut the deal on his new vehicle, a much more practical truck. He continued waiting for it to be prepped so he could drive it home. The salesman who had helped him was a young man who didn't seem to have much experience as a car salesman, which made the transaction relaxing. Reggie was aware of the other more seasoned salesmen, who appeared to be somewhat jealous. They had apparently misjudged him, assuming that he was only looking and not a serious buyer. Their faces hinted at their internal discomfort as Reggie completed his test drive and parked next to his black *Mercedes*. As he reached for his keys, walked over, and opened the door to show the young salesman the condition of the interior, as well as to verify the odometer reading, the young salesman beamed with excitement. As they walked back to start the paperwork, the other salesmen couldn't help themselves and stepped forward as they passed to eavesdrop. When they overheard Reggie confirm that he wanted to trade in his car that had no lienholder, the group of salesmen exchanged looks of disappointment over the missed opportunity.

Once they entered the sales room to begin the paperwork, Reggie explained that he had received the car in an inheritance from his best friend. But now he felt that it just wasn't his style. To the great pleasure of the young salesman, Reggie elected to pay full sticker price. He never even negotiated. He also bought the extended warranty and opted for the upgraded alarm system. It was the biggest cash sale on the lot for the month.

As the new fully loaded 4x4 *Dodge Ram* 1500 pulled in front, Reggie met the young salesman, who handed him the keys, along with a large envelope containing a spare set of keys, the sales documents, and the owner's manual. He also handed him a check. The value of the *Mercedes* far exceeded the purchase price of the truck, so he still had money coming back from his trade in. As Reggie drove out of the parking lot, he adjusted his seat and began driving to the graveyard. He wanted to tell something to Jonathan—well, to Jonathan's grave. Reggie wanted to explain why he did it.

* * * * *

Reggie parked his new truck on the surface road that ran between the aisles on the graveyard grounds. He parked it so that it was in direct line with Jonathan's grave. Ever since Reggie had met the attorney and finalized his inheritance, he had made it a weekly Saturday afternoon ritual to bring a fresh bouquet of flowers. After seeing the movie *Rocky Balboa*, he even started bringing a folding lawn chair. Reggie would clean any debris from the grave and the surrounding area before sitting down. Then, after sitting next to the grave, Reggie would have a one-way conversation intended for Jonathan.

Today would be a special conversation. Reggie knew he had to explain why he traded in the *Mercedes*.

"It's me again, Mr. Weed. I've brought another fresh bunch of flowers. I hope you like them." Reggie said as he leaned down and pulled the old ones out and replaced them with the new ones. "Things have been great for me. My parole agent has been super supportive about me going to college. I'm starting Junior College first until I know for sure what I want to do. You know that my parole agent knows all about the inheritance you gave me and wants me to keep it a secret from my mom. I never brought your car over to their house when I visited, I just rode the bus. I didn't want them to think anything weird." When he brought up the subject of the car, Reggie looked at his feet, pausing before he continued.

"I hope you don't mind, but I traded in the *Mercedes*. It just wasn't my style. I got a new pickup truck instead. You'd love it, Mr. Weed. I've parked it over there so you could see it," Reggie continued, as he pointed to his new truck. "It's a beaut, right?" he joked. Each visit, Reggie would end his one-way conversation by revisiting what he'd done at the wedding.

"Again Mr. Weed, I want you to know how I appreciate everything you've done for me. Without your help, things would sure be different. And again, I'm really sorry about what I did at Hye-Jin's wedding. I'm sure you understand. I know I promised and everything, but I couldn't do it. Or, I couldn't do what I thought you wanted me to do. I know that you never said it out loud or anything, but...."

Reggie hated suggesting that Mr. Weed had asked him to kill that Cameron guy, especially since he had never really come out and said it. But given what had happened, he wanted everything to be clear. After a brief pause, Reggie continued speaking.

"Like I've said many times before, it wasn't my place. The Cameron guy never did anything to me or my family. The other time, when I did do it, I didn't mean to. It was an accident. I was just trying to get the guy away from my baby sister. My counselor at Susanville told me he was probably a strung-out junkie like my mom was, and probably was as fragile as a twig. We just used the cover story of him being my uncle to protect everyone. But this Cameron guy, that's something I couldn't in my right mind do. I know you understand, but still I wanted you to know how I feel. And... I at least forwarded Hye-Jin all of the information you had on that guy. I'm sure she got it. I paid a dishwasher at the reception hall a hundred bucks to make sure she got it. I checked back the next day and he said she had."

Glancing across and speaking directly to Jonathan's grave marker, Reggie continued. "He told me that the Cameron guy slipped and fell anyway and died. So in a weird way, he got what was coming to him anyway, right?" Reggie stood up and turned away from the grave. He was finished speaking. He closed the lawn chair and paused. Unlike prior visits, when he had sensed Jonathan's presence, this time it felt empty, like he was speaking to himself. As Reggie walked back to his truck, he thought this might be his last visit for a while. He had been holding a similar weekly discussion for a year and a half. As Reggie climbed into his truck, he could see the fresh flowers on Jonathan's grave reflecting in his rearview mirror. As he pulled away from the curb, heading back onto the surface-gravel car paths along the aisles, he made his mind up. He would only come back on the anniversary of his passing. That way, he could share what had transpired over the last year.

As Reggie came to the main entrance to the cemetery, he looked at the large cross on top of the church. It reminded him of the large cross that hung in the church where Hye-Jin's wedding was held. He said a little prayer of thanks as he turned back onto the main road. He knew that there must have been some divine intervention that day. He had originally planned on doing it. But for some reason, after seeing that cross at the wedding ceremony, he couldn't bring himself to follow through. Reggie adjusted his sunglasses, breathed a large sigh of relief, and looked forward to his drive home.

# 23

Mike had been nursing a tall iced coffee, with his elbows resting on the table as he sat in a metal mesh chair outside of his local *Starbucks*. The bright afternoon sun required dark sunglasses, even in Nebraska. As Mike adjusted his glasses, he heard an annoying buzzing sound as a mosquito flew near his head. As Mike concentrated his hearing and purposely kept his arms still, he was able to see the black insect stop and land on his left hand. Mike waited for the mosquito to stop. He wanted to time his attack to take place just when the insect started to relax and began to extract a meal from Mike's flesh. After a brief pause, he swung his right hand down and smashed the bug with his palm. Turning over his right hand, he could see the bug flattened out with a bright red spot of blood. After wiping his palm on his pants, he noticed a bump begin to rise on his left hand. He had waited too long before attacking.

A young attractive woman was watching Mike. She stood up from her table and began walking back inside. "Did you get him?" she asked Mike with a perfect smile.

"Oh, yeah," replied Mike in a confident reply. Looking up at the woman, he noticed her diamond earrings. They appeared to be less than half a carat each. Glancing down to check her watch, he saw she had a higher end Seiko. It was okay. Then he glanced down at her purse and his heart skipped a beat until he got a better look. He knew right away that the *Louis Vuitton* purse was a copy. The stitching gave it away.

Smiling back at the woman, Mike's gaze drifted past her shoulder to where he could see his car. He had parked it in the center front parking space like he always did, ever since he came back from LA. This spot assured that everyone would see it. He even made a point of going back into the car whenever attractive women were around. He wanted everyone to know that was his car. He smiled to himself as he thought back to his return from LA, when he found a large crated package that had been left on his front porch. It was a miracle no one had taken it.

He had been stressed from doing all of the surveillance and then sneaking into the wedding. What would he have done if he'd been caught? Arriving home, Mike wasn't prepared for what he found. He had to push the crate through the front door. It was very heavy. When he located his hammer from his storage closet, he was able to pry off the top, where he found two unusual items: a metal-framed religious poem poster and a cat sculpture. The sculpture looked like wood, but upon touching it, he discovered it to be cold and metallic. After tilting the crate on its side, he rolled the sculpture out and struggled to hoist it onto his coffee table. He picked up the framed poster and laid it onto the kitchen table. As he dumped the packing bubbles out onto the floor to break down the crate, he found the letter, a note really, that Lee, a.k.a. Cameron, had written.

When Mike saw the letter, he picked it up, opened it, and began reading. There were only a few sentences. It read:

Mike,

I'm sorry for how things turned out. I can't change what happened. But if I could change it I would. I wanted to return some of your sister's most prized possessions.

My deepest apologies,

Lee Fullem

When Mike realized who had written the letter and who had sent the crate, he threw the letter on the ground and stepped back. His face twisted in revulsion. It was like Lee had reached out and touched him from the grave. He was still tormenting him through death. Contemplating the note, he stared at the seemingly worthless flea market items. It was like Lee was mocking him even now. As Mike stared at the stupid cat sculpture, something exploded in his mind. Without thinking, he turned sideways toward the sculpture, lifted his right leg to a bent position, and tilted his upper torso. As the muscle memory from his youth, taking those Tae Kwon Do lessons, took over, Mike coiled his leg up and with a quick focused thrust outward away from his body, he side-kicked the sculptured cat. Knowing the weight of the object, Mike had aimed at the base of the sculpture. The force catapulted the metallic object off the coffee table, sending it flying across the living room. It struck the paver-brick fireplace hearth, and the thinner top section of the sculpture broke away from the impact. With his eyes bulging, he stood in his living room preparing to yell at the top of his lungs. Catching his breath, he glanced down at the damaged sculpture, and the contrasting colors between the dark-brown paint exterior and the bright shiny gold inside caught his attention. The sudden intrigue and surprise defused his anger. Like an explorer who had just found a treasure map, Mike was drawn downward as the sculpture begged for a closer examination.

Mike picked up the broke top section. His thoughts began running wild. Maybe Lee had been sincere about being sorry. Mike suddenly switched emotions and went from rage to excitement. The emotional rollercoaster was overpowering. Using the same hammer he'd used to open the crate, Mike took the top sculpture section, laid it on the paver brick, and drove the hammer downward, breaking off several small rock sized chunks from the sculpture. Examining each piece, he could tell that the bright heavy metal was actually gold in color through and through. On a hunch, Mike took the rock sized chunks and broke them into many smaller pieces. He then took the smallest piece and put it into his pocket. Right away, he did a *Google* search on his smart phone and located a local pawn shop that also advertised converting gold to cash. Within minutes, Mike was in the car, following his GPS directions.

Upon arriving, he explained to the pawn shop manager that his father had found some chunks of gold debris during the war. After years of convincing him, his father had agreed to allow him to take it to be authenticated. To his shock, Mike learned that it was ninety-nine-point-nine percent pure gold with a trace of paint. Mike chose to convert that sample to cash and received four thousand, five hundred twenty-four dollars in cash. And he didn't have to report it on his taxes, either. Upon learning what Lee had sent, Mike sat in the parking lot and did some quick research on gold.

After watching several YouTube videos, Mike learned what was necessary to smelt the gold at home. He stopped by *Lowes* on his way home and purchased everything he needed. Heading straight home, he began a week-long project, reducing the sculpture down to a hundred twenty-eight small cast square bars, five ounces each. In order to avoid being tracked down once he began selling off the gold, he decided to rent a studio apartment in a different city. Using that location, he changed his address on his driver license. Once he started making more sells, he used that new license and never ever set foot near the studio apartment again. He simply mailed in his rent payments and made sure all the utilities were paid. He didn't want any of the gold buyers getting any funny ideas, trying to see if he had any more gold to sell.

To date, he had sold twenty of the bars. He had visited cities throughout Nebraska and in parts of Eastern Wyoming. He never visited the same place twice. He had been so focused on the gold that it had taken several months before he discovered the hidden stolen painting and diamonds. He had a good feeling about the heavy picture frame but he hadn't yet had it analyzed. He had plenty of time to do that later. With his converted gold money, he purchased a used white *BMW* 755LI. Also, given his increased visits to pawn shops, he found several opportunities to upgrade his wardrobe to include a used *Rolex* President yellow-gold watch. His newfound wealth had sparked a previously unknown preoccupation with outward materialistic items.

Mike was brought back to the present as the young woman spoke again. "Excuse me. Do you know where the restroom is?"

"It's down the hall to the right," he said. Then, sarcastically, he added, "Oh, and be careful. Those floors are slippery." With a shifty grin, Mike picked up his drink, walked over and got into his *BMW*. Then he drove away.

\*     \*     \*     \*     \*

The custodians were busy in the lower level, clearing the room. It had once been an outdated abandoned conference room that the hospital staff had converted to a temporary art studio for Miss Kim. But now, with her departure this evening, they had been instructed to clean and clear the room. Her living quarters had already been cleaned and readied for another new patient, but not the art studio. It was getting late. There was no sense of urgency, so the custodians enjoyed looking at her paintings. It almost felt like they were in an art museum. Miss Kim had confirmed that she didn't want to keep any of the paintings. As such, management decided that each custodian who wanted to, could take one painting home to keep. It was the first perk that these workers had received from working here. There was a sense of excitement within the workforce as they took turns going down to pick a painting. For most of the employees, that area had been considered off limits.

"Wow, look at this one. Isn't it beautiful?" said one of the morning shift custodians. She had stayed later after her shift had ended so she could pick out a painting. "This would go great in my living room."

"I like that one too," said the male custodian who had just arrived for his evening shift. After hearing the news, he ran down to make his selection before they were all gone. "Look at her newest one. I wonder who it is?" he said.

Everyone in the room stopped and stared at the portrait of the man. He had a mustache and a shocked expression on his face. "Huh?" said one of the custodians usually assigned to the cafeteria. "I wonder why it's signed. None of the other paintings are."

"I never noticed that." He leaned down and studied the Korean hangul written characters. "Hey, Sandy?" he said, raising his voice so she could hear him from across the room. She was the only Korean who worked there. Sandy turned her head away from a beautiful seascape she'd been studying and walked over to the portrait. "What does that mean?" he asked, as he pointed at the picture. "Is that her signature?"

Sandy looked at the script and raised her eyebrows as if surprised before she spoke. "No, it isn't her signature. It's the Korean word *michaso*. It means 'crazy.'"

All the custodians present stared at the painting and had similar reactions. With their arms folded in front of their bodies, several custodians' only remark was "Huh? That's strange." After a brief pause, they each turned their backs to the portrait and continued searching for the painting they each wanted to take home.

Greg had already been to his locker and retrieved his phone charger. The traffic had been minimal and his drive back was uneventful until he arrived in the parking lot. As he exited his car, he saw several other custodians carrying Miss Kim's paintings to their cars. After hearing the news, he made his way down to the art studio. He passed many other custodians in the hallway, each carrying a single painting. By the time he arrived, only two paintings were left: the portrait and one last painting still hanging on the wall.

Greg glanced around the now empty room. All the other custodians had picked the place clean. Everyone had left. He was alone. Locating a wall outlet, he plugged his phone charger into his cellphone and then inserted the prongs into the outlet. Urgent to see the photograph of his niece, he waited for the battery to get enough of a charge to start back up. After it had rebooted, he accessed the photos. After he located the photo, he opened it up and touched his fingers to the screen and began zooming in to get a close-up view. As the picture enlarged on his screen, he was grateful that it had come out clear and in focus. Greg smiled at the picture, too distracted to realize the significance of that moment. If anyone else had been in that room, and had seen the picture he had just taken of his niece, they would have recognized it as a perfect match of Hye-Jin's painting that hung on the wall. The baby in the center appeared to be a girl, surrounded by two boys. Their blue and her pink colored name tags matched up as well. One of the baby boys was even much larger than the other two babies. It was all the same.

Greg exhaled a powerful breath, one signifying the end of a long, productive day. As he unplugged his charger from the wall, he felt grateful. Now, while he slept, he could charge his cellphone. Before he walked through the doorway, he turned back toward the empty room. Maybe it was the emotional high he had experienced from his niece's birth, or maybe it was the exhilaration of his new job. But, for whatever reason, he felt different—more connected, more confident, more sure of himself. He was certain that his life's path was on track. He was where he was supposed to be. Before turning and walking out the door, Greg spoke.

"I wish we had spent more time together. I could tell that you were special. You've made a difference in this world. I wish you could have shared more with me." Without thinking, he bowed downward from his waist. As he rose back into an upright position, he said, "Good-bye, my princess. Good-bye."

# About the Author

A first Generation Filipino on his father's side, Padilla was the last of four children born in the US and raised in Red Bluff, a small town in Northern California. Padilla attended UC Irvine, majoring in Physics, and ultimately graduated from CSU Sacramento with a Bachelor of Arts degree in Economics and a minor in Psychology.

Prior to writing, Padilla was employed in the banking and insurance industries. He has one son, who aspires to be a touring professional electric guitarist, and a stepson who is involved in the voiceover recording industry. Padilla currently resides in North County San Diego.

# Other Books by the Author

E. A. Padilla's first book is titled **Rule One Twenty**. This exciting tale of suspense, murder, and intrigue follows the main character, Curt Anderson, as he uncovers a secret government agency that coerces citizens into following its agenda or facing the ultimate punishment. This journey starts out along the mountainous and picturesque Highway 17 that runs toward the Santa Cruz beaches from the San Francisco Bay Area. From the very beginning, the reader learns how the finely tuned, well-organized Agency handles its business. After Curt's discovery, he feels compelled to share this knowledge with the only person he thinks he can trust, his girlfriend, Melody. . As one reviewer put it, "International leaders, stateside bigwigs, and simple common folks are all potential targets as we are taken on a wild ride of twists and turns, mystery and murder."

Padilla's third book, **Tunnels**, is scheduled for release in the second quarter of 2017. It's an action thriller surrounding a family split between North and South Korea, whose future hinges on the actions of a U.S. Marine who **discovers** a brother using underground tunnels to travel back and forth between these two opposing countries.

Padilla's fourth book is **Sentinel Event**, the sequel to **Rule One Twenty**. It will be completed the last quarter of 2017.

Visit the author's website at www.eappublishing.com to learn about his future projects and book-signing events.

www.ingramcontent.com/pod-product-compliance
Lightning Source LLC
Chambersburg PA
CBHW051654260626
47170CB00004B/1495